Jessica's Vampire Diary

BOB SAENZ

A RED SKY PRESENTS BOOK

Cover Design by Jerry Todd

ISBN: 978-1-941015-74-2

Published by Red Sky Presents
A Division of Red Sky Entertainment,

I really am sorry there was such destruction, but it couldn't be helped. Stinky told me early on that property damage was probably going to be necessary. I try to be responsible. I really do. I know people work hard for the things they have. Dad and Mom tell me this all the time when I break something of theirs, so the wreckage bothered me. Honest.

Not as much as almost losing my family.

Now that I think about it, I think what Stinky really said was, "Anytime you're dealing with the undead, it's going to get messy."

For the record, since this is kinda official, at least for me, my name is Jessica Trueheart Scott. Yeah, Trueheart. It's from my mom's family someplace in the past. I'm not sure exactly when. She told me once. Maybe a great grandfather who was in a war and did some stuff? That sounds right.

It still sucks as a middle name no matter where it came from.

Mom blamed Grandma, but I'm old enough to know Mom signed the birth certificate. Mom still said that Grandma "suggested" it for my middle name. Mom makes air quotes when she says "suggested," so there you go. Has the name Trueheart caused me to get into some fights at school from time to time over the years? Okay. Yes. I'm fourteen years old now and at that age you still can have a fight over funny middle names, but mostly it's yelling now.

My friends call me Jess, by the way, because I hate the name Jessica. Jessica sounds like an American Girl Doll name and I never played with dolls. People kept giving them to me and I kept playing games where their heads somehow got separated from their bodies, so Mom made me fix them and then she took them and gave them away. A lot of them had the wrong heads on them.

I like to play with anything that has some action involved. I once talked Patty Ann into building a bike jumping ramp when we were eight. After that, Patty Ann couldn't play with me anymore. Anyways, only Mom can call me Jessica, but she never does. She understands. Dad always called me Jess. Lily calls me "Ick-a," but I think that's just to torment me.

I live in Centerville, a semi-small town way up north in California not far from the Oregon border with my father, mother, a little sister who is almost five (and not altogether human either, if you ask me), and my dead grandmother's dog. We live in a semi-nice four-bedroom house on a court not far from downtown. Well, one of the bedrooms is really my dad's home office. My dad is an engineer at a computer type company up here. Okay, it's not computers, but something inside them and I'm not exactly sure what he does there and he doesn't bring home any samples. I should be more interested in what he does. That's my bad.

My mom works at home. She used to work at a place where they did the taxes for giant companies. It was one of "The Big

Four." Or Five. I know this because she tells anyone new we meet about it. They all seem to understand it.

We moved here from Los Angeles (yeah, I could be living in Hollywood) when I was nine and Mom was pregnant with Lily. After we moved, Mom decided she should be a mom at home. She keeps telling me it was her choice, so I know it's not expected of me, that I get to make my own choices about my life. Except most of the time she doesn't like the ones I make and tells me "No" a lot.

When I tell her they're my own choices, she says, "When you grow up, you'll understand." My friends tell me their moms say the same thing to them. I guess there's a moment in your life when, BAM, you get it. Like you're playing Mario Cart or something and WHAMMO, you understand what your parents meant by everything. That's what it sounds like.

School is really important to Mom. She always talks about going back to school herself. Not to get another degree, she says, but just to improve her life. That amazes me. Wanting to go to school when you don't have to? Weird. Anyways, that's what caused her problem in the first place. And why Stinky and I almost got ourselves killed. Dead.

I go to Centerville Junior High School. Well, not anymore. I went there when all this happened, but we graduated last month and now I'm going to go to Sally Ride High School in the fall. They call it "The Sally" around here. Mom told me Sally is famous for being the first woman to go to space in the olden days. Mom didn't say olden days, but since women go to space now all the time, it must have been. Mom said Sally paved the way for me to go to space. I really don't want to go to space, but still, I think that's pretty cool.

I'm not a brainiac, but I do okay. I'm not on the honor roll, but my grades are good enough so my parents don't bug me too much about them. Unless I get a D. Which I did once. Mom was pretty upset about that. Dad told me to never do it again, but I think it was more about Mom's reaction than it was about me.

There are lots of kids in all kinds of groups at my school. I'm not in any one of them. I don't belong to any clubs or sports teams. I'm for sure not one of the "popular kids" at my school at all. In fact, there are a lot of times, okay . . . most of the time . . . where I felt invisible except for my friends and of course, Rocco. Which most of the time is fine with me. I'm certainly not the kind of person who calls any attention to themselves. I do have friends and everything, but at school unless I'm fighting someone over my middle name or the one time I stood up to Rocco, which until later was a huge mistake, I'm one of the vast herd of kids that no one much remembers later.

This is me. Or was.

I was pretty much nothing to write home about. Until I was forced to act. And believe me, I was.

And I'm not afraid to say it out loud. I love my mother.

It all started last January 1st.

For the record: This is the official diary of my adventure, for all of you taking notes. This last part is a joke because Dad says I can't ever show this to anybody as long as I live and that it's for myself only, to get it out of my system. He says I'll understand some day. So, I guess it's one more thing I get to understand in the future. It all started on New Year's Day.

January 1.

My dad wanted to spend the whole day watching football. I wanted to do . . . well, nothing. I stayed up until, like, one a.m. to watch the year change. It was okay. It didn't feel any different. Mom and Dad kissed, like real kissed, in front of me and I got to taste some champagne. Tickled my nose, but I don't know what the big deal is with it. It's kinda sour.

Anyways, doing nothing can be fun, especially when you're tired. I don't even get bored doing nothing sometimes. But . . . you don't use the "B" word in my house. I learned that early when I told Mom I was bored and she made me weed the whole yard. I've never said it again. I've been coaching Lily to say she's bored because she doesn't know what happens yet, but so far, she keeps forgetting to say it.

Mom gave me the side eye when I said I was doing nothing. "I can't sit around and do nothing," she likes to say, "I have things to do."

Actually, she had important things to do. She was going to my grandmother's house. Grandma was really sick. Not stay in bed sick, but inside sick with cancer.

I told Mom I'd go with her to help if she wanted me to, but she said she was afraid I wouldn't be able to take it if Grandma looked bad. That would have made sense if she hadn't planned to take Lily along with her. I mean if Grandma looked all mashed up or something, Lily would freak for sure. Lily couldn't even stand to look at Grandma's dog. But then, neither could I.

January 3.

Grandma died on New Year's Day before Mom could even get to her house. I knew Grandma was really old, like sixty or eighty or something, but I never knew anybody who died before. I mean, knew. People die. I know that. But Grandma was family. And even though we never really got along, unlike most kids who get along with their grandmas, I felt bad for Mom, who didn't get along with Grandma all that good either. Mom was sad anyways. It was her mom. I got that.

So . . . when Mom got to Grandma's, she saw police cars, and ambulances, and firetrucks. An awful lot of flashing lights. She called Dad to come get Lily so she could stay. Dad told me Grandma fell over dead in her backyard with some neighbors there. Dad said that Mom didn't need this right now. I told him I'll bet Grandma didn't need it right now either. He got mad at me, after he kinda laughed.

So, me and Dad went and got Lily. Dad didn't even complain about missing his game, because going to help Mom was important. Dad's like that. He knows when to complain and when not to. He's good that way. That's what Mom says.

Dad is . . . well, Dad. Some of my friends hate their dads right now. I don't know what their problems are, but I like my dad. When I tell my friends that, they think I'm crazy. But he's funny and explains stuff to me before he tells me no. I still don't like it, but at least I know why. Plus, he doesn't yell. Well, not as much as some of the other dads, according to my friends. And as horrible as I have been sometimes? That's pretty good.

Anyways, we got to Grandma's and all the cars and trucks and vans were still there. Mom and Lily were out front waiting for us. Mom carried Lily to the car and put her in the back seat.

"You want me to stay with you, Mom?" I asked.

She held up her hand. She didn't say a word. Just held up her hand. Her eyes were all red, too. She looked Dad in the eye and Dad said, "Your Mom needs to take care of business and needs to be here alone, not to be worrying about you, too."

Mom kinda half smiled at me, nodded at Dad, and turned and walked back to the house. Never said a word.

It was then that my brain got all disconnected from my mouth and I said to Dad, "Why is she crying? All she did was fight with Grandma."

Don't get me wrong, I'm not being disrespectful or anything, but like I said, my grandmother and Mom didn't get along that well. This was for always, according to Dad.

My mom has four sisters and Grandma raised all of them by herself. I never knew my grandpa, but a couple of years ago I heard Mom telling my father that her dad had called her and that she'd hung up on him. She was mad. Like steaming mad. I never saw her that way ever, not even the time I put the hamster inside the piano.

Mom turned out great as a person though, so I figure it was

better that Grandma raised the girls alone without Grandpa. I also have no idea why Grandma and Mom fought. When I asked, Dad said it was "complicated." That's a word parents say to their kids when they don't want to explain something.

I fought with Grandma, too. I know why we did. She asked me all the time why I didn't wear dresses and girl shoes instead of jeans and sneakers. I told her because I'm not a dress kind of girl.

But that's not true either. I have some nice dresses and some girl shoes that don't hurt too much, and I do wear them when I have to, but when I don't? I don't. Why wear stuff you don't want to wear? Mom got it. She never made me put on girly clothes unless I had to.

Grandma once bought me a dress that had so much lace and bows and frills it looked like a dessert instead of a dress. And I think that's what I told her in an earlier moment of brain disconnection. So, she never gave me anything else after that, even on my birthday or Christmas.

Well, not until after she was dead.

The only person Grandma really liked was her dog. She had a fat Welsh Corgi named Whitman. She told me she named him after a dead poet or something. But hey, she really loved that dog, that lazy disgusting dog. All he did was beg for food and sleep. And fart. On me. Every chance he got.

And he couldn't sleep unless he had his nose in one of Grandma's shoes. It was gross. That's why I always called him Half-Whit. Grandma didn't appreciate that very much. It may have also had something to do with the no presents thing. Anyways, she kept trying to get me to like Half-Whit, but you couldn't fool me—that dog was a waste of space.

To his credit Half-Whit could do one trick. Only one. Grandma spent years teaching him to open the drapes. I have no idea why; it seemed like a stupid trick to me. I mean, if you're going to teach a dog only one trick, jumping through a flaming hoop is definitely better. He finally did learn the drape thing though.

"Whitman, sunlight!" Grandma would yell from her big yellow overstuffed chair in the living room, and that dog would jump up, grab the end of the drapes, and drag them open. Okay, it wasn't a bad trick for a low-slung squatty dog like Half-Whit. But as much as I tried, I couldn't get him to do it for me. I would sit in Grandma's chair and scream at him to open the drapes.

Nothing. Like I wasn't even there. He didn't even move. I couldn't even get him to take his nose out of Grandma's shoes. I finally stopped trying.

Let me be real clear on this. I hated that dog.

Anyways, I could tell Mom had still been crying when she came into my room that night after she got home. Her eyes were still all red and puffy. I felt bad for her. She always takes care of us. I wish I could have taken care of her this once. She sat down on my bed and put her arms around me.

"Jessica," she said.

Uh oh, I thought. She called me Jessica. That is never good.

"I know you and your grandmother weren't very close, but she loved you very much. The last time I saw her I think she knew she didn't have much time left. She told me she wanted you to have her most prized possession when she passed away."

Okay. Maybe she wasn't as mad at me as I thought. My thoughts were instantly about money, or jewelry I could sell for money. Or maybe I got Grandma's car. Yes! A car! Or the house! The house . . . cool. I could sell the house and buy . . . anything! I think I was lost in thought when Mom spoke again. It was then I got sick to my stomach.

"Whitman," she yelled out the door, "here's your new owner."

Yep. Grandma was still mad at me.

Plus, that dumb dog even came with his own box of Grandma's shoes.

January 7.

A bunch of us were standing around the football field at school. I think we were supposed to be exercising for P.E., but Coach was over talking to Miss Hawkins, so we were goofing around.

Well, everyone else was goofing around. I was thinking about Mom. She was trying to take care of us and trying to take care of Grandma's business. And . . . she was still moping around. I wanted to make her feel better, but accepting Half-Whit was taking it too far. So, while I was lost in thought I missed all the signs of an impending Rocco attack.

As I wandered away from the group, Rocco stuck his foot out and tripped me. I hit the ground hard. There was a lot of laughter from the other kids. Rocco required it or they were next.

You have to understand something about Rocco. He was an equal opportunity bully. Big or small. Girl or boy, or anybody. Even the teachers. He didn't care. As long as he was making someone's life miserable, he was fine.

It was then that I made what was my possibly fatal mistake. I jumped up and shoved Rocco. I think I said, "Screw you, Rocco." The audible shock from my friends brought me back to the real world and I think I saw my life flash before my eyes.

His eyes weren't too happy, either. A girl had challenged him. A girl. In the crowd, someone giggled. That wasn't good for me.

Maybe now's the time to further explain Rocco Semona. Rocco is big. I mean, big and hairy. The rumor was that he'd been held back so many times that he drove himself to Junior High. He wasn't called One Punch Rocco for no reason. He had no problem sneaking up on anyone and sucker punching them into oblivion because he felt like it. And the school never did anything about it. I think they were afraid of him.

Anyways, no one had ever gotten him back, so what happened next Danielle told me was kinda semi-legendary.

First, he tried to grab my ponytail, which is kinda long, but I moved and he missed. Then, Rocco took a swing at me. Told you he didn't care if I was a girl. I ducked that too and instead of running away like a smart person would, I punched him flat in the nose as hard as I could. It started bleeding, too. Rocco grabbed his nose and, I'm not kidding, started to cry. "My nooosssse. My nose!"

Then he stopped crying and looked at me. "Trueheart," he

said, all scary calm and stuff, "you're dead." All the bullies called me that after they found out it was my middle name. Something I had to live with.

Once again, I didn't run away like I should have. I guess all the frustration with Mom and Half-Whit and Grandma all hit me at the same time and I decided to commit suicide by Rocco. I put my fists up.

"You think so?" I taunted. "You think so? Come on. Let's go." Obviously, I was completely insane.

Rocco's nose was still bleeding as I advanced on him. Rocco, shocked, backed up just a little, stopped, got madder, if that's possible, and raised his gigantic fists. Danielle told me later that if they hadn't banned cell phones from P.E., the video would have been on YouTube before the second punch.

But the fight never happened. Me and Rocco must have been more interesting than Miss Hawkins because Coach grabbed me before anything else happened. "Okay. That's enough! Break it up."

Next thing I know I'm sitting in Principal Fellows' office with Mom. Rocco wasn't even around. How fair was that?

"Mrs. Scott, I'm sorry for your loss. And for Jessica's loss, but that doesn't excuse this kind of behavior."

Okay, yeah. I used dead Grandma as an excuse for fighting before Mom got there. It didn't work.

Principal Fellows was looking oh-so-serious. "And Jessica will have to serve some kind of detention."

I guess I was still not myself because I didn't shut up and

take it. "Oh, come on. Give me a break. Rocco must have hit two hundred kids this month alone. He's never ever gotten detention. And it was self-defense anyways."

The look on Principal Fellows' face was great. I didn't give him a chance to get over the shock. "You probably already know that," I said. "Anyways, Rocco always hits first."

Mom, who was trying really hard not to smile or maybe even laugh, looked fake sternly at me. "Jess! Shush. Be happy. Thank Mr. Fellows for not suspending you." I knew it was fake sternly because she didn't call me Jessica.

I looked at him. "Thank you for not suspending me." I didn't mean it, and he knew I didn't mean it. But he took what he could get.

As we walked out of his office, Mom looked at me. "Anyways isn't a word. Please stop using it. It's anyway, no s. Okay?" Then she walked out and left me there. I had to run to catch up with her.

On the drive home, she didn't say anything for a while. When Mom didn't talk, it was never good. Finally, at a stop sign, she said, "I don't need this right now."

"Yeah, I know. I'm sorry, Mom." I should have ended it with that. I didn't. "But he took the first swing." I winced, waiting for her reaction. I didn't get the one I was expecting.

"Promise me we won't have any problems so big we can't work them out."

"What?" That wasn't close to what I expected.

"Promise me." She looked like she was going to cry.

Then I got it. This wasn't about me. Or Rocco. It was about Grandma. And the fact that she and Mom never got along. Mom was feeling guilty. That's when I finally felt really bad about what I did. Then I remembered Rocco probably was going to kill me soon. "I promise." I said to her, knowing I probably wouldn't be living long enough to worry about it.

January 8.

Half-Whit had been around for a week and all he'd done was sleep and beg for food. And fart. Gee, big surprise. He also hung around Grandma's shoes a lot, even when he was awake. I know he misses her. And hates me. Mom even suggested that I take him to Grandma's funeral today. Thank goodness Dad said he didn't think that was a good idea. I was in a kind of panic thinking about being seen with that dog in public anyways.

So, we went to Grandma's funeral without Half-Whit. Good thing too, it was hard enough as it was. Mom cried, Lily cried, but Lily always cries, so I don't know if she knew what was going on or what. Mom's sisters were all there and they cried and hugged and talked, all at once. I felt bad because I didn't cry, but I almost did when Mom did. Almost.

Yes, for those keeping track, I wore a dress. Mom bought me a new dark blue dress. And she fixed my hair up. Since we wear the same size shoe (okay, I have big feet), she asked if I wanted to wear a pair of her high heels.

She does have one fancy pair I played with when I was little, but just to knock down Lego walls and stuff. They have these cool wooden heels. Mom yelled at me because they were really expensive.

Oh . . . and I said no thanks. I tried high heels once. It was like those toys that wobble, but I did fall down.

We got to the church and there weren't too many people there, but Mom said lots of Grandma's friends were dead, too. So, it would be family mostly. But the place filled up later because I have like a zillion cousins.

In the church, Mom grabbed my hand when one of her sisters was up talking about Grandma. Not hard, but really gentle. She looked down at me and smiled, then back up and started crying again. It was then I really got what she meant about not being mad at each other ever. Was it one of those BAM moments where I understand everything? I don't know. Anyways, I know it sounds weird because we were at a place where Grandma was in a box up front, but I never wanted Mom to let go of my hand. But she did, finally.

I asked her why she didn't go talk about Grandma up front.

"You'll learn that it's better to say nothing when you don't have a lot of good things to say." Great, more things I'll understand later.

"You could make some good stuff up," I whispered.

"No, honey. That's not the way it works."

It's junk like that that makes me love my mom more.

There are kids at my school who talk about how crappy their moms are. Most of those kids are pretty crappy themselves, so I'm not sure if it's just them, or if it's their moms' fault. Mom and me have our disagreements, but she's always trying to hear my side of everything before really getting mad. That's pretty good. Like I said before when I wrote about Dad, I have done some pretty stupid stuff we don't need to get into. For example, like fighting Rocco.

After it got dark, we went to a kind of party afterwards, except Dad said it wasn't a real party. He said it was a "get together" to honor Grandma. Which I was glad about because a party for dead people doesn't seem right. At school, we do this thing in English class about words that don't go together, and "dead Grandma" and "party" are pretty good examples. I'll have to remember that one. It'll make Miss Clarkson give me the evil eye. Grace and I have a bet on who can get the most of them this semester.

Anyways, the "get together" was in a big room at the old State Building downtown.

When they built the new State Building a couple of years ago, they turned the old one into a kind of city community center thing. The bottom floor is a big room you can rent for stuff like Grandma's party. Upstairs was the new adult night school. The top floors were turned into some apartments the teachers could rent if they wanted to. That's what Dad said. He thought it was a good way to make the old building pay for itself. I have no idea what that means.

I also think part of the deal was that the night-school teachers had to take care of the place too, because some of them were working at Grandma's funeral party that night. Dad liked that too. He said it made "good business sense." I think he tells me stuff like that thinking I understand it. I just nod yes, even when I don't.

Once we got to Grandma's party, Mom took off to thank all of Grandma's friends that were still alive and to spend time with her sisters. Dad made me look after Lily. That was the only time I wished we'd brought Half-Whit. It would have been better to watch that stupid dog than to have to watch my sister, who decided that day to act like an out-of-control tornado.

Lily spent the entire time running around and getting in everyone's way, and Dad kept blaming me. He couldn't have done any better than me keeping up with her that day. She finally ran into one of the waiter/teacher guys and almost knocked him down. He didn't get mad; he just asked that I keep a better eye on Lily. In fact, all the waiter guys were almost like robots, kinda. They didn't really talk to anyone, they just glided around the room serving and cleaning.

Later on, I noticed one of them staring at my mom. He was a pale, thin guy with black hair and black eyes. I don't mean dark brown, I mean black. And not black eyes like he got socked in the eye, like Rocco did with Kenny, but his eyeballs. Black. It was weird, so I got as close as I could—once—and made sure. He saw me looking at him and kind of smiled. It wasn't really a smile, he just showed me his teeth. It gave me the creeps.

So, I dumped Lily on my Aunt Irene, who loved it and kept hugging her, which served Lily right, and I spent the rest of the night moving Mom away from that waiter, who was kinda following her around, I think.

It got so bad, I couldn't take it anymore and grabbed my Mom.

"Hey, Mom . . . that guy is staring at you," I told her, while he was doing it.

"What guy?" she said.

"That guy," I said back, pointing to creepy man.

Mom pushed my hand down. "Don't point . . . and yes, I saw him. And he's not staring at me."

"The hell he's not," I said, grabbing my dad. "Do something—now."

Mom swung around and looked at me, "Did you just swear?"

I shook my head "No." She just sighed and turned away. For my mom to not yell at me for my language? She was having a really bad day. Dad wasn't so forgiving. He grabbed my arm.

"Jess, don't bug your mom. Today is tough enough without you getting weird on her."

"So, you're not going to do anything about another man staring at your wife?"

Dad smiled."That's what you get when you marry someone as amazing as your mom. Been happening since I met her. Don't worry about it."

Oh, ewwww.

But then I remembered Kenny saying he got picked to play in little league even though he sucked at baseball because the coaches liked how his mom looked. I don't know what I think about that, but it sounds wrong to me. People shouldn't get an advantage by the way they look. Or how their mom looks. Doesn't sound fair.

I looked at Dad. "Just stay with her, okay?"

Dad leaned down to me. "Jess, here's a little life lesson for you right now. Good relationships are built on trust. Your mother is the most trustworthy, smart, capable person I have ever known. Man or woman. She's fine. So, stop it and go find Lily." He walked away.

"Well, I still don't like it," I said under my breath. I turned to go get Lily, but the waiter guy started moving closer, all the while staring at Mom. When he got too close, that was it. I said to Mom, "Hey! There's Aunt Jackie! I haven't hugged her yet," and I grabbed Mom's hand and dragged her away from him.

Mom turned to all the people in earshot, and said loudly, "Please excuse my no-manners daughter." Then she turned to me and said, "Do you even know which one Aunt Jackie is?"

Do I? Kinda, but that didn't stop me.

I must have hugged a million aunts that day keeping Mom away from that guy, but he kept on staring at her. I was glad when we left that night, even though the guy came out on the steps up to the building and watched us go.

I saw him. He saw me see him, too.

Dad may have been okay with it. I wasn't.

January 15.

Lily got a new little bike on her last birthday. Dad finally got around to teaching her how to ride it. Or at least he tried to teach her. She had a lot of trouble learning without the training wheels. My dad isn't a patient guy with stuff like that. Even though I was inside the house, I could hear Lily screaming at him from outside and Dad finally yelling back. That's when Mom went out and sent Dad into the house. Lily was riding the bike in no time.

Later, Dad and I were standing on the front porch watching Lily ride like a pro. Dad sighed and said, "Jess, the way it was going, Lily was going to be still trying to learn how to ride. And I would be dead. Your mom comes out, says a couple of quiet words to her . . . and voila! She's ready for the Tour de France."

Of course, then Mom, who is always trying to get everybody to exercise, suggested that we all take our first all-family bike ride, now that Lily could join us.

"You're on!" yelled my dad. Then he turned to me. "Tour de Scott. You haven't got a prayer," and he took off running to get his bike. I love a challenge, plus I knew I could slaughter him in a bike race.

We got on our bikes and rode off. As we headed downtown, I raced out in front of everybody. I got so far ahead, I decided to stop for a drink of water and wait for Dad and rub it in. When I got to the old State Building, I stopped and waited for them. It was all closed up. Ever since they'd started the night school, the building was always locked and dark during the day. It seemed like a waste to not use it during all those good daylight hours. Wait—I thought that? I did.

Wow . . . maybe Dad's business stuff is rubbing off on me.

While still on my bike, I leaned over and took a good long

drink at the water fountain.

As I waited out front for my slow family to catch up with me, some movement in the bushes on the side of the building caught my eye. Something was in there. I got off my bike, propped it against the fence, and walked over to see. It was then that this kid jumps out like he's shot out of a cannon and hits me square in the face with a water balloon.

"Die, you blood sucking creep!" he yelled. Then he ran off around the back of the building. I didn't get a real good look at him with all the water in my eyes, but I could tell you he was a kid I'd never seen before. Maybe. The water made my eyes blurry.

Just then, my family arrived. Perfect timing. "What happened to you?" my father asked as I stood there before him, dripping wet.

"Some kid hit me with a water balloon," I said as I bent over to pick up the pieces of broken balloon to show him.

"Is this someone you know?"

"No. Never seen him before."

"What gets into these kids?" my dad asked.

"Beats me," I said. "But if I see him again, he's a dead man."

"Don't talk like that," Mom said. It was then that Mom asked the standard Mom question. "Did you do something to cause this?"

Parents always think everything is their own kid's fault. You could be sitting on your lawn and a plane could crash right on you, and your mom, while sifting through the rubble looking for you, would say, "Did you do something to cause this?"

"Mommmm . . ." I whined, but she wasn't listening. She was

looking at the front of the building.

"You know," she said to my dad, "I'm glad we stopped here. I've been meaning to talk to you about me taking a class here at night."

"What kind of class?" he asked.

"Hey, I'm all wet here," I said.

My dad gave me a dirty look and turned back to my mom. "What kind of class?" he asked again.

"Oh, an art class or a writing class. Just something to challenge me a little." As she was talking, her eyes never left the front of the building. Mom didn't need a challenge, I thought. Raising Lily and me should be enough. I waited for Dad to tell her no.

"You know I'll support you in anything you want to do," he said to her.

I couldn't believe it. Plus, he never said that to me. I wanted a motor scooter like Wendy has. Think he said yes? Not on your life.

"You know," I said, "I'm soaking wet here. Can we go home?"

Mom stopped looking at the school and looked back at me. "Oh honey, I'm sorry. Let's get you into some dry clothes."

So, Mom and Lily rode off home. Dad stayed while I got my bike. Then he said, "Come on."

"Dad?" I said, although I wasn't entirely sure why I was saying it. "I don't want Mom going to school here. Hasn't she been to enough school already? Who volunteers to go to school anyways?"

Dad shook his head at me. "Part of being a family is each one of us making sure that others have what they want. Your mom loves school, so that's what I want for her."

"I love not being in school," I replied. "Could you want that for me? And the motor scooter thing would be nice, too."

"And I love you pulling weeds," he said back, smiling.

"Good point," I answered. "Let's go home. I'm cold."

As we rode away, I turned back and looked at the old building. There was something telling me Mom should stay away from it. It gave me a chill. Or maybe it was the wet clothes.

January 26.

Football Playoff Sunday. I watched with Dad. And I played a video game on his phone. I can't wait until high school starts, and I get my own cell phone. I get kidded about that a lot. Everyone else in the world has a cell phone. Not me. Dad and Mom said I had to wait until high school. I think they thought I'd never get there. Well, it's coming soon and I'm getting a phone.

Dad says he's gonna get me a cheap flip phone, but I think he's kidding. He better be kidding.

Mom came in once, while the game was on, with her night school catalog. She wanted Dad to look at it with her, but her timing wasn't too good. The game was close and exciting, and Dad couldn't look at anything else right then.

"I'll pick something by myself," she said. Then she looked at me. "Unless you want to come look at this with me?"

I may have made a face. Okay, I made a face. Mom put her hand up. "Okay. I got the message."

"Uh, what?" said my dad. Mom shook her head and left to look at her catalog.

Looking back, we should have paid more attention to Mom.

February 11.

Kenny sat down with me at lunch. "Rocco's gunning hard for you today."

"Well, duh. I thought that was every day," I told him.

"But he doesn't usually tell everyone. He's telling everyone."

I shook my head. "I don't wanna know."

"You better. And you also might want to write your will out in fifth period. Oh—can I have your laptop when he kills you?" Kenny laughed. I think he was half serious though. Kenny's laptop is really old.

I ignored him and took a bite of my sandwich. Or tried to take a bite. I bit down and came out with a piece of folded paper in my mouth. I took the mustard covered paper out of my mouth.

"Okay," I demanded. "Who put this in my sandwich?"

Everybody just looked at each other and denied it. Danielle said nobody would want to touch my food. Everybody laughed. Except me. Kenny said, "What does it say?"

I opened it up and in big lettering and in crayon, it said:

STAY AWAY FROM THE OLD STATE BUILDING

I looked around to see who was watching us. Nothing out of the ordinary. I looked at the note again.

"Come on! What's it say?" Kenny grabbed for the note. He missed. I stuffed it into my pocket, mustard and all.

"Nothing. Just forget it."

Kenny made a grab for my pocket, but the bell rang and we had to go to class. Whew.

I must have looked at the note a lot that afternoon. My hands were so yellow from the mustard by sixth period that Mr. Matthews wanted to know what I'd gotten into. I think he knew though. I smelled like mustard by then, too.

Before I went home, I washed my hands. Then I snuck off campus, careful not to let Rocco see me.

When I got home from school, Mom was making dinner. "Isn't it a little early for dinner?" I asked.

"It's for later, honey. You'll have to reheat it. Tonight's my first night of class."

Class? I had totally forgotten about Mom wanting to go to night school. She was still serious.

"You really going?" I asked.

"You bet. I've registered for a class on European art. It should be interesting."

"European art? Come on, Mom. That's about as interesting as watching Half-Whit sleep. I don't know why you need to go to school again. It's just a waste of time."

Uh-oh.

As soon as I said it, I knew I'd made a big mistake.

"I'm surprised at you," she said. "You can never get enough education." I knew that was coming. "I just want to improve myself and it's only one night a week. Is one night a week too much to ask for myself?"

I felt guilty and terrible. Mom supports all of us and is involved in everything me and Lily do. It never occurs to me that Mom might want to do something just for herself, and even though I knew about the night school thing, I never thought she'd actually do it. I guess it helps if I remember that she's not just Mom, but a person, too. That's hard to do sometimes.

So, while Mom was gone that night studying European art, Dad reheated dinner for Lily and me. After he put Lily to bed, I asked him if he minded Mom going to night school.

"Sure, I do," he said. "Only because I miss being with her. Not because I don't want her doing anything on her own. That's not how good relationships work. Your mom needs her own free time to do things for herself. I know I also need time to myself—sometimes. Anyway, it's not up to me to decide what's best for her. All I can do is be supportive and help around here so she can go to class without worrying about the rest of us." He sounded just like Mom.

"Don't you worry about her being out alone at night?"

"Of course, I worry. I worry about all of you all the time. She's a grown woman. She can take better care of herself than you think." But as I went to bed, I saw him looking out the front window, waiting for her to come home.

February 14.

Valentine's Day. Ughhhh. Mom put some mushy card in my

lunch and all my friends saw it. Including Rocco. He grabbed it and tore it up and laughed at me. I laughed too, because Rocco socks you in the eye if you don't. It's a good thing we were in the cafeteria and the school security guy was there, because he wanted to sock me in the eye anyways. "You can't hide from me forever, Trueheart," is what he said, throwing the bits of card in my face.

Kenny gave me a Valentine. I think he was expecting one back. I mean, I like Kenny. But not like that.

There was one boy I liked. Julio. And he moved away. So, I think I'm waiting for another Julio. We almost kissed once but his brother messed it up. I don't know why I'm telling you this.

Anyways, I didn't give Kenny a Valentine. I can't figure why they set aside a whole day to be all lovey and stuff. Makes no sense.

Plus, Mom and Dad kissed all morning long. I thought that they were too old for that unless it was New Years.

February 18.

We took Mom to night school. I had to go to the library to do a report because our internet was down and we don't have books about Central America at home, so Dad said he'd take me and drop Mom off at school on the way. I said I could do it on his phone, but I think he wanted to check out the school. So going to the library was a good excuse for him to do it. To tell the truth, I'm glad he wanted to check it out.

Mom wouldn't let Dad walk her to class. She said she was

late and would run up alone. Except we weren't late. Dad knew it too but didn't say anything. Dad told her we would be waiting in the parking lot when her class was over. I don't think she even heard him. She just nodded and ran off into the building. Dad just shook his head. He stopped when he saw me watching him.

I had to go to the library because I had a report due the next day and couldn't put it off anymore without getting an F. Well, to tell the truth, I kind of forgot about it until my social studies teacher said, "Your country reports are due tomorrow." And then the internet went down.

I told Dad I guess I couldn't do it and maybe he could write me a note for school saying that, and he said, "That's what libraries are for." He's too smart for me.

I had one night to find out all I could about Honduras and the library was gonna have to do. Dad also said I had to do it by myself because I had waited so long, and this would teach me a good lesson.

"Give me a break," I said. "Please help me with this and I'll learn my lesson on some other report." I smiled hopefully at him.

"Sorry, kid," he said, smiling back. "You're on your own."

"At least tell me where Honduras is."

"Okay," he said, as he left with Lily to find the children's section. "It's southwest of here."

So, I spent the evening learning all kinds of things about Honduras that I'm sure I'll need later in my life. Right. It's like, they call their money lempiras. Lempiras? How many lempiras for a Big Mac and fries? When I grow up, I'm sure some guy is going to walk up to me and say, "If you can tell me what they call their money in Honduras, I'll give you a million dollars."

Well, I finished my report or, to be honest, the encyclopedia finished my report. The internet would have been so much easier, but no. And there's no copy and paste at the library, so my hand was tired, too.

Dad came back a few times with Lily to see how I was doing, but he still didn't help me. He didn't want to read the report when I was done, either. I think he felt guilty for not helping me. Plus, he knew he'd have to spend the rest of the night rewriting it with me.

After we left the library, we stopped for ice cream, then went to wait for Mom. Her class was two and a half hours long. I didn't think that there was that much European art. After a while people started coming out of the building.

"Classes must be letting out," I said.

"I hope Mommy got me a present," Lily said. Little sisters haven't got a clue.

"Oh yes, Lily, "I said. "Your own collection of European art. Or a poison apple." She's been watching what she calls The Snow Dwarfed Movie a lot lately. She screamed. I got a great deal of satisfaction out of that.

"Jess, cut it out," my dad said as he tried not to laugh.

All this time, people were coming out of the old State Building in droves, but still no Mom. I could tell Dad was starting to get a little upset. As it got later and nobody else was coming out, I could tell Dad was close to going in after her.

"There's Mommy!" shouted Lily. She was pointing to the lobby of the building. Sure enough, Mom was in there talking to somebody. Dad rolled down the window and let Lily go on yelling for her. Mom must have heard her because she came out, but she wasn't alone. She came out with that same creepy guy from Grandma's party. The same guy! The same guy I tried to keep her away from. The guy with the black eyes. I couldn't believe it. I had to do something.

I jumped out of the car and ran to intercept her. "I'll get her," I yelled back to Dad. As I got closer to them, I could see they were in deep conversation. I heard all I needed to.

". . . you'll need some special attention," the creep was saying to Mom.

"Mommy. Mommy," I yelled. Mommy? I sounded like Lily.

"Jess," she said, still looking at him, "this is my art teacher, Stefan." Oooo, he even had a creepy name. "Stefan, this is my daughter, Jessica."

Jessica? Are you kidding me? What was going on here?

"You're a very pretty girl," he slimed. "Very honored to meet you." He held out his boney hand for me to shake. It was the coldest hand I had ever felt. I'd have bet Grandma's hand was warmer and she's dead. I had to get Mom away from there.

"Mom, it's late and Lily and Dad are waiting in the car." I said that so Stefan would know my dad was there. "And it's way past Lily's bedtime." I hoped Mom would buy my fake concern for Lily.

"It is getting late," she said. "Well, goodnight, Stefan." I tugged at her arm. "Okay, Jessica—we're going." Jessica again? Holy crap. Plus, she was talking to me, but she never took her eyes off him. "I'm looking forward to next week."

"As am I," he said. Then he turned and looked straight at me with his cold black eyes shining. "And it's a good girl that looks after her sister like you do." He had me figured out already. He didn't buy my fake concern for Lily at all.

"Goodnight, Jessica," he said to me. Then he looked into my mom's eyes. "And goodnight to you, Sandra." I took Mom's hand and pulled her back to the car.

"Sandra?" I asked. "What's this 'Sandra' stuff?"

She gave me one of those Mom looks. "I'm not in the fifth grade. Adults do use first names. What's wrong with you anyway? Why were you so rude?"

"I don't like that guy. He was the one staring at you at Grandma's party. Doesn't that bother you?"

"Jess, this conversation is over," she said, coldly. At least she called me Jess.

"Who was that?" my dad asked, as we got into the car.

"Just my teacher," Mom answered with a little giggle. "He kept me after school for talking in class." Mom sure was acting strange. Dad didn't say a thing, but I'm sure he was bugged. I know I was.

When I got in bed, I could hear Mom and Dad talking. I couldn't hear what they were saying, but I could hear they weren't having fun. I didn't like it. It wasn't a fight because they never fight. It was a conversation, but the tone wasn't the best.

Half-Whit didn't like it either. He sat, just looking at the door like he was listening too. Then he fell over on his side.

As I lay there, I knew I had to find a way to keep Mom away from that guy and that school. To do that, I had to find out more about Stefan. As close as Mom and I are, I knew she wouldn't listen to me unless I could prove this guy was creepy and maybe dangerous. I just didn't know how to do it.

February 21.

Saturday. Today was the day. It was time to go check out the old State Building. I had to feed Half-Whit first. He was begging for food again. I fed him. He begged for more food. I fed him again. He begged again. I threw him one of Grandma's shoes. Then I got on my bike to leave. I told my parents I was going to the park to meet Danielle. I knew Danielle was out of town, so my parents couldn't call her. It was a brilliant plan.

As I rode over to the old State Building, I started thinking about what I was going to look for once I got there. I decided I had no idea.

When I got to the front of the building, I found it closed and it was dark inside. I locked my bike to a tree and walked up to the glass doors. The lobby was dark and empty, and I could feel a cold breeze on my feet from under the door, right through my tennis shoes. I put my hand down and just about froze my fingers off. It felt like the air conditioner was on high. In February? How could anybody live in that kind of cold?

I decided to check out the rest of the building. I walked completely around it a couple of times, trying every door. All locked tight. As far as I could see, there was nobody at all inside. Maybe if I could see into one of the upstairs rooms, I could learn something. Anything.

At the back of the building were some old oak trees. I decided to climb one and try to see inside from there. First, I made sure no one was around, then I climbed the one closest to the building. I got up in it far enough to see into a second-floor window. I had to focus hard to see into the dark room.

From what I could see, it must have been one of the classrooms. It looked like a science room. There were lots of big bottles with tubes running out of them sitting on a table. It was too dark to see what was in them. Again, there was nothing at all moving inside. You'd think with people living in the building you would see someone in there or find at least one door that opened to the outside for them to come and go.

I moved up in the tree to try and see into the upper two floors. All the windowpanes were painted black. Why would anyone paint their windows black? I was thinking about that when I heard a noise right below me.

I looked down and saw a kid sneaking around the side of the building. He had a backpack on and was carrying two big shopping bags. The kind with the handles. From where I was, I could see that they were filled with balloons. Balloons? WATER BALLOONS! It was the same kid who hit me. Was he there to ambush other unsuspecting people? I didn't know or care. I had him now.

I watched while he set up his stuff in the bushes. He pulled a small blanket out of his backpack and spread it on the ground. Then he took out a big jar of what looked like sand and poured a circle of it around the blanket. It was fascinating to watch. He did it with such precision, a complete circle with no breaks in it. This was not a normal kid.

He took the shopping bags one at a time and placed them on the blanket, each time stepping carefully over the line of sand so he wouldn't disturb it. Then sitting in the middle of the blanket, he reached into his backpack and pulled out a kind of a gun. Yeah, that's right. A gun. It didn't look like a real gun—it had that orange tip the fake ones have—but it didn't look like a water gun either. Water balloons is one thing, but a gun? Hey, this was serious. I knew I couldn't chance a surprise attack on him now.

He set the gun at his feet and pulled out a pair of binoculars. Mentally, I said a prayer: Please don't look up here. Luckily, he didn't look my way at all. He was focused on the building.

Not wanting to take any chances, I must have sat up in that tree for hours. I don't know because I don't have a cell phone to check the time and even though I have a bunch of watches, I don't wear them.

Anyways, the kid didn't move from his blanket, so I didn't move from my tree. As it finally got dark, I could see shadows of people moving inside the building. Ah ha. So, there were people in there. But it was Saturday, so there was no night school, and these people were moving around on the classroom floor. Especially in that science room. It was weird too, because they never turned on the lights.

I was getting cold, and my legs were cramping and I had to go to the bathroom, but that beat maybe getting shot at by some nut. And he was still there.

Soon it was so dark I couldn't see my friend in the bushes anymore, so I assumed he couldn't see me. Just in case, I still moved very slowly out on the branch toward the science classroom window to get one better look inside, before I got out of there. Trying to make out what was going on in there was difficult. As I tried to focus, I saw a human outline in the window. Suddenly, it turned and looked straight at me.

Actually, all I saw clearly was a pair of glowing red eyes.

I know it sounds like maybe I'd been in that tree for so long I was seeing things. At first, I thought so myself. So, I closed my eyes, cleared my head, then opened my eyes to see two pairs of glowing red eyes looking right at me. My only thought at the time, besides being more scared than I had ever been in my life, was, "I have to go now."

With no thought of the guy below me in the bushes maybe having a gun, I got out of that tree. I don't even remember how I got down. By some miracle, he didn't hear or see me. The next thing I knew I was running through the bushes as fast as I could, trying to get to my bike. I wrestled my bike lock key out of my pocket, unlocked my bike, left the lock and chain on the ground, and rode out of there. I didn't even look back.

My parents were waiting outside when I rode up.

"Where the devil have you been?" my dad yelled, only he

didn't say devil. "You scared your mom and me to death. We were ready to call the police."

I was still frightened from what I had seen, but I had it together enough to know they would never believe me if I told them the truth. I don't like to lie, though. Then, I decided I couldn't tell them the truth anyways because I was spying on Mom's school and that creep teacher. So I concocted a story about my bike being stolen from the park and me finally finding it across town. It was pretty lame, but it sure beat the truth.

Well, after a lot of lecturing from my parents, I apologized for not calling to get their help or telling them what was going on. I even used the whole thing to suggest they get me a cell phone right now. My dad laughed and said, "Nice try."

We all made up and they hugged me and fed me, happy I was safely home.

Once I got to my room, I took off my tennis shoes and WOW, what a smell. I mean stink city. Bigfoot's shoes wouldn't smell this bad. I picked up one shoe and poured out what looked like sand. I must have run through that kid's circle of sand trying to get out. I picked some up in my fingers and smelled it. I knew that smell. Garlic? He was pouring garlic on the ground? It was too confusing to try and figure out. I threw my shoes in the closet and tried to go to sleep. My mind kept going back to those red eyes in the window. Were they real? Was it all a dream?

I was exhausted, but I didn't know what to make of all I had seen. I did know, however, that inside the old State Building there was some major weird stuff going on.

The last thing I remember seeing before I finally dozed off was Half-Whit sleeping in my closet, with his nose in my garlic tennis shoe.

February 24.

Mom went to that class again. Dad paced the floor waiting for her to get home. He said he wasn't waiting for her, that he was just feeling restless, but I knew better. I considered telling him about the glowing red eyes in the window of Mom's school and the kid who was hiding in the bushes outside her school and the garlic in my shoes, but he'd insist there was probably a logical explanation for it all. Or he'd laugh at me. Not good either way, because I'd look stupid.

I would also be admitting to him that I had lied about my bike. Lying to Dad is like the most horrible thing you can do. He once told me, "I can understand and cope with anything you do or don't do, but if you lie to me, all bets are off. You understand?"

So, I tried really hard never to lie to him. And now, what have I done? I lied to him. Now if I tell him the truth all he'll hear is that I lied. Talk about digging a hole for yourself.

Mom came home even later than usual.

Worse yet, she came into my room after she got home and sat on my bed. "Are you awake?" she asked.

The way she had been lately, I almost faked sleep, but thought better of it and answered, "Yeah, Mom. What's up?"

"My art teacher, Stefan—you remember him, don't you?"

Yeah, I remember that slimy jerk, I thought.

She didn't even wait for my answer. "He took me aside after class and told me he saw you climbing in the trees near the night school. Is that true?"

Oh, boy. I had to think fast. This really threw me. I couldn't tell her I was spying on him.

"I was trying to find my bike after it got stolen," I answered. Good thing I can think of stuff quick, even though it's more lies I shouldn't be telling.

"Up in a tree?"

"No, not in the tree. I thought I could see farther looking for it from the top of the tree." I knew she would never believe me. I started sweating. Not a good sign of truthfulness.

She didn't even notice. AND she bought the story. Was this MY mom?

"Well, that's very dangerous," she said. "Stefan was worried something could happen to you. He told me to tell you not to do it again. He's doesn't want you to fall."

"Gee," I said. "Sounds like he's real concerned about me." It didn't NOT sound sarcastic. I must learn to control my mouth. Or at least the way I say stuff.

Now she was mad. "Look, he didn't have to say anything. He could have just let you get hurt. Don't do it again." She got up and left. She didn't say goodnight or anything.

I knew the truth. Stefan just didn't want me snooping around. All the more reason to find out what's going on in there and why my mom was acting so strange.

I lay there for a while thinking about what she had said. So,

Stefan was concerned. How wonderful. But I still couldn't figure out how he could have seen me there unless. . . unless . . . oh, no . . .

Oh, yes. Stefan had the glowing red eyes!

I didn't sleep that night.

March 3.

My birthday. Officially fourteen.

And I had sort of a birthday party. Mom didn't pay much attention. She's always given the best birthday parties, but not this time. She didn't forget it. That would be like scary to the max. She kissed me and said, "Happy birthday," then said something about schoolwork. I did get some presents. Dad gave me a new pair of tennis shoes. He must have smelled the old ones. Now, I could give the old ones to Half-Whit. He's grown attached to them.

Lily gave me a coloring book. Oh, boy. She must have thought I was turning five.

Mom's present was a real surprise. A book. And not just any book. An art book. Repeat, an art book. This thing was going too far when it started affecting my birthday.

March 4.

At lunch time, I was sitting outside on the lawn at school with a few other kids, when I felt someone come up behind me. "Hi there," a voice said. "Climb any good trees lately?" I turned around and saw the kid from the bushes.

"You knew I was up there?" What else could I say?

"Listen, I know more than you would believe," he answered.

"And I know you're nuts," I said. He showed no reaction.

"Look, I've been checking you out and you've got trouble. We need to have a serious talk," he said.

"What do you mean, 'checking me out'?"

"Do you want to know what's going on right under your nose, or not?" I felt my nose. Don't ask me why.

"What are you talking about?" I looked at the other kids for some support. They had no clue either.

The kid ignored my question. "Meet me after school, downtown. At the library."

The library again? What's up with that place? I thought.

I never even had time to say no to him. He left as fast as he came. I turned to my friends and asked, "Any of you know him?"

Rochelle spoke first. "I think he's in my English class, but I don't know his name." She said she thought it was Edgar or Louis or something like that. She said he sat in back and never said anything.

Kenny thought he might be in his P.E. class but wasn't sure. I told Kenny that I was in his P. E. class, and I knew for a fact that guy wasn't in the class. Kenny just made a face.

"Well, I tried," he said.

No, he didn't.

No one else could remember ever seeing him before. Great—it was like this guy didn't even exist.

I went straight home after school and told Mom I was going

to the library, and I added that she should call the police if I wasn't home in two hours. She just laughed and didn't ask why I'd be going to library. The Internet was fixed a long time ago. That was just plain weird. So, I left.

Riding to the library on my bike, I kept thinking, Am I making a big mistake meeting with this guy?

Well, at least it would be in public so he probably wouldn't try anything. Also, he said he'd been checking me out. Why? And what did he mean when he said I had some trouble? I had lots of questions for him.

He was waiting out front when I got there. He was shorter than me and probably weighed like forty pounds more than me. His dirty blond hair looked like it had been combed maybe once, right after he was born, and then never again.

He was nervous and jumpy, not a good sign for a guy you know might have weapons. I told myself to be careful. I locked my bike and went to meet him. I didn't give him a chance to say anything. He'd had the advantage long enough.

"Okay," I said. "Obviously you know who I am. Well, I have no idea who you are. Nobody at school knows you. So, if you want anything from me, you're going to have to tell me who you are and what the heck is going on."

Wow. I sounded almost like my parents.

He held out his hand for me to shake and smiled. "You don't have to be afraid of me. You've got enough other stuff to be afraid of."

"What the heck does that mean?" I asked. "Afraid of what?

Who are you?" I also didn't shake his hand. He held it out until he figured I wasn't going to, then scratched his head to hide the fact I didn't shake it. Didn't make his hair look any better.

"Let's go inside. I'll explain everything." He opened the front door of the library and motioned me in.

He headed straight for the Adult Fiction Section, went down a book aisle, stopped at the "S" section, bent down and took a big paperback book out of the rack. He motioned me to a table, and we sat down. He threw the book down in front of me. "Recognize this?" he asked.

I turned the book over. In large letters on the front, it said, *Dracula*. It was by Bram Stoker.

"You mean like the late-night horror movies?" I asked.

"No, I mean like real life. That book in front of you should be in the non-fiction section. It really happened."

"You're talking about Dracula, right? The vampire? The guy from Transylvania who sucks the blood from people's necks and turns them into his vampire servants? Then, he turns into a bat and flies away? That Dracula?"

"Exactly" he said. "I'm glad I don't have to explain it to you."

"You think Dracula is real?" I started getting up to leave because this guy was completely nuts.

"I can prove it. Sit down and listen to me."

"Prove it?" I repeated. "This I've got to see." I sat down, not believing him at all, but it was too strange not to want to know what he'd say next. It didn't take me long to come to my senses though. "Wait," I added. "You can't prove that. Are you on crazy pills? Is this some kind of TV show where they punk you?" I asked. "I'm getting out of here." Then I finished getting up to leave.

"My name is Abraham Van Helsing the Fourth. It was my great-great grandfather who killed Dracula. Not a fiction Dracula, the real Dracula. Please sit down and I'll tell you about it."

I stared at him. He looked and sounded so sincere. It was like a dream. If it was a dream, it was too weird to wake up from yet. I sat back down.

"Okay, Abe," I said. "Go for it. Convince me."

"My friends call me Stinky."

Stinky? Well, he did have the faint odor of garlic about him. Plus, he has friends?

"Okay, Stinky," I said. "Go for it."

He looked around the library to make sure no one was listening, then moved his chair closer to mine. He did smell like garlic.

"My family, the Van Helsings," he said, pointing at the novel in front of me. "Like in the book, they have been rooting out and killing vampires for generations. My great-great grandfather made the mistake of telling his story, the Dracula story, to some guy in a bar in London in the late 1800s."

"Let me guess. This Bram Stoker guy?" I asked, reading from the book cover.

"You're pretty smart. Yep, took the whole story and wrote a bestseller. And most of it is true."

"Most of it?"

"Yeah," he said. "Stoker made up the part about them turning into bats. They can't turn into bats. Everything else is true."

I had finally heard enough. "This is insane. What makes you think I'll believe anything you say?"

"You'd better. Your mom's right in the middle of a whole bunch of them. She's going to the night school, right? What better way to hide that you're a vampire than as a night school teacher?"

Okay. My brain was now on spin cycle. I needed some air. This was too weird. Time to wake up if this was a dream.

He continued, "Vampires can't go out during the day. Sunlight destroys them. If you think about what you saw from the tree, you'll know I'm right. You can't see anything moving in there during the day. The windows on the upper floors are blacked out. The whole place is only open at night. And those eyes that sent you out of that tree weren't movie special effects."

I knew I was in trouble. He was starting to make sense. But vampires? Here? With Mom?

No way.

"Hey—no. There's got to be a logical explanation for all of this. You need one of those psycho doctors." I jumped up and pointed my finger at him. "You're a sick boy."

It was like he didn't even hear me. "Vampires live in small family groups," he said. "The vampire in control has recruited or turned all the others in his group. He has enormous power over them, but once in a while one of his family members grows powerful and challenges the leader. That vampire either defeats the leader or is sent off to start his own family. That's how the night school got started."

"A new leader?" I asked. I sat back down and leaned in.

"My dad says it's a guy who was sent away from a family in London. He started the family group at the old State Building a couple of years ago when the building was sold to the city. From what my dad can figure, this leader has recruited ten or more guys to serve him. Mostly it's people with no real family or criminals with nothing to tie them to anything. Or vampires from other families that have come to serve him instead. All people who won't be missed. They only survive by not drawing attention to themselves, but occasionally the leader will find somebody he wants even if they do have a family and ties to the community. And that's why I'm worried about your mom."

Oh, wow. It got me thinking. That creep staring at Mom, the freezing air in the building, the hand that was colder than my dead grandmother. *Oh no*, I thought. *It's Stefan.* Stefan is the leader guy. The Chief Blood Sucker!

I moved even closer to Stinky. More garlic smell. "It's my mom's art teacher, isn't it?" I said, hoping I was wrong.

"Not too hard to figure out, is it?"

"Wait a minute," I said. My brain nerves were firing all over the place. Jess calling real world. Come in real world. I swung my head around to make sure no one was within hearing distance. I think I hit him in the face with my ponytail because he was waving his hands around when I looked back at him. "Don't vampires have to drink blood to stay alive?" I had him now.

"Of course they do," he said.

"Well, I know I don't keep up with news that much, but I'm sure I would have heard about a bunch of people in town here with all their blood sucked out. Everybody at school would be talking about it and making jokes. And I don't think there's a drive-through window at the blood bank." Logic wins again.

"Listen, these modern vampires are real smart," he said. "Back in old times, even as recently as a hundred years ago, when people died young, you know, and didn't live as long as they do now, vampires could just go out at night and kill a few for their blood. Sometimes they got caught and got a wooden stake through the heart, but mostly they got away with it. Not now. No way. They couldn't hide it if they wanted to. Today, there's the Internet, Instagram and CNN."

I cut in. "Killing them with a wooden stake is true?" I see that in a lot of vampire movies.

He hit himself in the head and rolled his eyes, just like I did when Lily said something stupid. "Haven't you been listening? I told you it's all true, except the bat part. Anyway, I was trying to talk about their blood supply."

"Okay, so where do they get their blood?" I asked, before putting my head down on the cold table.

"There are other ways to get blood. They have it down to a science. They even post advertising all over town every three months for it."

I lifted my head. He had my interest again.

"I'm sure you must have seen 'em," he continued. "I even think I've got one here somewhere." He reached into his backpack and fumbled for a moment. "Here it is," he said, and dropped a piece of paper in front of me.

I picked it up. It said in big letters on the top:

COMMUNITY NIGHT SCHOOL
QUARTERLY BLOOD DRIVE

Help save lives.
Make sure Centerville has all the blood
it needs for any emergency.
Free coffee and donuts
Balloons for the kids
Hours: 8:00 pm to 11:00 pm
his Thursday, Friday, and Saturday Night

YOU CAN'T AFFORD NOT TO COME
a critical blood shortage affects us all
DO IT FOR YOUR COMMUNITY AND FOR YOUR FAMILY

I couldn't believe it. Vampires who advertised for blood? I thought about it and hey, why not? Maybe Stinky was telling the truth. This guy was convincing me that there were vampires in the old State Building. Plus, free donuts.

"Okay, so they get their blood every three months, put it in the fridge for later, and all without killing anybody. No big deal," I said.

"It is a big deal. These guys live for power. This Stefan is not a nice, sweet guy. My dad has a whole file on his laptop on this guy. First, he takes over the night school, now he's asking the city if he can help run some of the nighttime parks and recreation programs. Then maybe some city business and bingo," he snapped his fingers, "he's running the whole show. Just what he wants. And, he has his eye on your mom."

"Stop saying that." I stood again and said, "I don't like it." He had me popping up and down like I was in a toaster.

"Like it or not, it's true, and we've got to stop him before he turns her."

"Turns her?" A zillion thoughts flew through my head. They stopped on one. "Like into a vampire?" I asked, a little too loud.

The librarian came over and told me to be quiet. For the first time since I got there, I was afraid someone in the library would hear what we were saying. I looked around. No one had heard a thing. If they had, they'd be calling 911. I sat down again and looked Stinky in the eye.

"How?" I whispered. "How can he turn my mom into a vampire?"

"Don't you know anything? All he has to do is bite her three times. It has to be over a certain amount of time, because if he goes too fast, it could kill her."

"How much time?" I asked.

"Two or three months, I think. Or maybe four, give or take a couple of weeks. But the victim shows signs of changing before the last bite."

"What kind of signs?"

"Fading out in the mirror a little, maybe. Vampires can't see themselves in the mirror."

"Okay, what else?" I asked.

"Oh, not wanting to be in the sun, no more Italian food. Stuff like that. And they don't know what's happening to them until it's too late. They just start acting strange."

"Italian food?"

"You really don't know anything, do you? Garlic. They can't stand garlic."

"You mean that's true, too?" I was having trouble breathing now.

"It's all true—all except for the bat part. I don't know where Stoker came up with it, but my family's gotten a lot of laughs out of it for years."

I had to get out of there. I jumped up one last time and ran out the main door. He caught up with me on the front steps. "Where are you going? I'm not done."

It was a good question. Where was I going? Then it hit me, so I turned and said to him, "I've got to tell my dad. He'll put a stop to this right now. Will you come to my house and tell him what you told me?" Without waiting for his answer, I started down the stairs.

He grabbed my arm, stopped me, and swung me around. "No way," he said. "He's an adult. They never believe anything like this. They look for logical explanations. They need proof. He's not going to believe some strange kid without finding out for himself and that would put him in as much danger as your mom."

He was right about the strange kid part.

"How?" I asked.

"First, he'll laugh at us. Then he'll tell your mom, who'll laugh at us. Then your mom will tell her art teacher, who'll laugh at us and then find us and do something unpleasant. Like suck all our blood out." He took my arm and led me out to the lawn in front of the library. We sat down on the grass.

"You have to understand," he continued. "These guys don't fool around. Most of the head guys are over two hundred years old. They have a lot to hide. They will eliminate anybody who gets in their way."

"Eliminate? Like, kill? They would kill my dad?" The thought of Dad in danger because of me was too much. I lay back in the grass and looked up at the sky.

"Well, they'd kill us first. Then your dad. That's why you can't tell your parents."

"You know, this is like the craziest conversation I've ever had in my whole life. Why should I believe you?"

"Hey," he said casually. "Don't believe me—at your own risk."

He was so matter of fact. So confident in what he was saying. I thought he was either totally bonkers or telling the truth.

"They usually arrange an accident of some kind," he added. "Mostly fire."

More thought. Do insane people go to these lengths? Putting warnings in sandwiches? Sitting in circles of garlic? Really? But I couldn't risk not believing him at this point. I sat up.

"Okay," I said. "So we can't tell my dad. What do we do?"

"We eliminate them instead. It's my family business. And because my dad is working in Russia for the next three months, I have to do this one on my own."

"Vampires are in Russia, too?" Wow—maybe his family was killing them around the world.

"No, he works for Levi's. He's there selling jeans. Killing vampires is more of a hobby for him. It really doesn't pay that well."

"A hobby?" I put my head in my hands. "It's a hobby?" I mumbled to myself. This had to stop. I looked directly into his eyes. "Why me? You said I didn't know anything about vampires anyways. I don't think I can help you. Maybe you should find someone else—"

He cut me off. "Listen to me. You're already involved. They saw you in that tree. They may think you know too much already." He took my arm again. "I need your help. I can't do it alone."

Then it hit me. Not in a good way, either. "Oh, man," I said. "You're right. Stefan told my mom about me being in the tree. They do know. He told her to keep me away."

"You think you have a choice?"

I had to decide. He was forcing me to choose. A story that couldn't possibly be true or that my mom was in grave danger. It was time to make up my mind. I decided in favor of me being just as nuts as him.

"Okay, I'm in for now," I said, giving myself a way out if this was all bull. "But if I'm going to help you, I'll need to learn all I can about those guys."

I just couldn't take a chance he was wrong. I needed to protect my family.

"Great. We can get started tomorrow."

"Oh, I can't tomorrow," I said. "I promised my dad I'd weed the backyard after school. I get paid by the weed."

Weeding sounded even stupider than ever now. My mom might be hanging with bloodsuckers that might turn her into a night-dwelling monster and I'm worried about weeding?

"Then the day after." He picked up his backpack and put out his hand. "Welcome to the wonderful world of the undead." We shook hands and he left.

As I rode my bike home, my mind went everywhere. Not on riding for sure. I'm not sure how I got home.

When I got there, the first thing I did was ask my mom for spaghetti and garlic bread for dinner sometime this week. She said sure. I felt better.

March 5.

Mom went to class again. I faked like I was getting sick to try and keep her home. All she did was give me some awful pink stuff to drink and then go to class anyways. Ewwwwww.

While she was gone, I wanted to tell Dad everything, but Stinky was right—if he was telling the truth and not just mental. It was too risky. I didn't want Dad to get hurt. If only I could get him to believe me without having to check it out for himself. But adults just don't do that too good.

I pulled the weeds in back. Every time I pulled one, I imagined I was killing a vampire. Dad said it was the best job I'd ever done.

Mom got home from class a little later than usual. I waited up with Dad. Kinda. I had to do a math project thing and needed the Internet, and he was in there watching TV, and sneaking looks at the computer to make sure I wasn't looking at crap I wasn't supposed to. Not funny videos or anything. We watch those together. Or the rock and roll live music, stuff he loves. Those are okay. But bad stuff.

He didn't think I saw him. I did. But honestly? Some of the stuff my friends find on the Internet and tell me about? No thanks.

March 6.

I got up excited about the day. This was the day I was going to learn about vampire hunting after school from Stinky—or I might be turning him in to the authorities if it turned out he was crazy. I reminded Mom about having spaghetti and garlic bread this week and she said she was planning it for that night. The day was working out great.

I got to school and waited for it to end. I didn't do too well on my math test, but I got my project turned in. I really wasn't paying much attention in class. I never thought this vampire thing would affect my grades. I hoped my teachers didn't ask me why I was so distracted.

Anyways, Stinky didn't show up after school. I looked all over for him. I was starting to get worried when a car pulled up in the school parking lot. The window rolled down, and the woman inside stuck an arm out and waved at me. "Are you Jess?"

Now, my mother had always warned me about talking to strangers, but since it was sunny and she couldn't be a vampire, I decided it was okay to answer. I played it cool anyways. "I can get her a message if you want me too."

"Could you tell her that Abraham has a cold and can't play today."

Can't play? She made it sound like we were five years old.

"I'll tell her," I said. "Thank you. Can I tell her when Abraham will be well enough to play?"

"He should be back in a couple of days. Thank you again, young lady." Then she drove off.

If that was his mom, she sounded like she didn't know a thing about what he was doing. I'll have to ask him about it, when he gets well.

The spaghetti was great, but Mom forgot the garlic bread.

Uh-oh.

March 8.

Stinky called on Saturday, after missing two days at school, and said he'd meet me the next day. He said he was sorry he got sick, but we'd really have more time on a Sunday; we'd have all day. I asked how he got our number.

"The Internet," he told me. "You do know what that is, don't you?"

"You want my help or not?" I asked. That was just insulting. But then again, he may have been seriously asking. He was so weird.

"Yes, I need your help," he said. "Please."

He said please, so I told him I would have to ask my parents, because Sunday is family day around my house.

The tradition for me is to ask to do something with my friends on Sunday and their traditional answer is always a look, that look, that please tell me you're kidding look every parent has, followed by a laugh and the word, "No."

This time? No look.

Just a shrug, and then my mom said, "Sure, honey,"

Mom didn't mind me going out at all? On Sunday?

She said she had studying to do anyway and for me to go and have fun. Mom had never let me go anywhere, except with our family on a Sunday. But worse? She didn't even ask who I was going to be with. Come on. Usually, I get questioned like the FBI is conducting the investigation. Not this time.

Was this the strange behavior Stinky was talking about? Had Mom been bitten already? It was time to check her neck.

That night we all watched a movie. It was about a bunch of nutty professional wrestlers who were also super spies. Dad picked it because it had wrestlers for him, and it was approved for kids, too. It was pretty lame, but some parts of it scared the heck out of Lily, so that made it entertaining enough for me.

While the movie was on, I squeezed in next to Mom on the sofa to check for bite marks, but it was hard. My mom has pretty, shoulder length hair, so it covers her neck pretty good. I tried all evening to get a close look at her neck, but I couldn't do it. She kept telling me to quit playing with her hair. Dad finally made me sit across the room. I'll have to find a better way to check her for fang marks.

March 9.

Sunday. I waited for Mom to change her mind about letting me go out, but she didn't. I gave her every chance. But no. This was getting serious.

On Monday, I got to the school early, but Stinky beat me there and already had his stuff set up on the football field in back. He had brought the water balloons, the gun-looking thing, and a big mayonnaise jar full of garlic powder.

He also explained about his mom. Part of the long tradition of his family was to not tell the women about this vampire hunting thing. So, his mom didn't know about him or his dad or their ancestors hunting the blood suckers.

"Hey," I asked him, "haven't you heard of equal rights? Women can hunt vampires, too. I'm a girl and you want me to do it. Mom is always telling me and Lily we can do or be anything we want. Like, there are no limits. I'm not sure about Lily yet, but I know Mom is right about me. "You should tell your mom about everything," I finished. "Maybe she can help."

By the way, I also believe girls can be anything they want to be. If I want to be a vampire hunter, I'll be a vampire hunter. I'll be the best vampire hunter ever. Wait. What am I saying?

"Like we told your dad?" Stinky asked, interrupting this thought.

"Oh—yeah," I said. "We'd need to prove it to her."

"If my mother thought I was out tracking vampires, she would never let me out of the house at night."

"What does she think you're doing?" I asked.

"Collecting bugs," he said.

"And that's okay with her?"

"Are you kidding? She has a bigger collection than I do," he said proudly.

I definitely have to meet his family. Or not. It was time to get serious.

"I'll bet you have some questions for me," Stinky continued.

"I do. I know about the garlic, but does it kill them?" I asked.

"No, they can't stand the smell. It drives them away. They can't be anywhere near it. It may even hurt them a little. That's why you should have some around. I'll bet your mom has some garlic powder or garlic salt in your kitchen. Just use that."

"Okay, I can do that," I said, and made a mental note to look in the kitchen. "In fact, I'd better get it before she throws it out. If Stefan has bitten her, she'll want all the garlic out of the house."

"You catch on fast, young lady," Stinky said. He was smiling.

"Now, tell me about the water balloons. I don't understand that at all."

"Ah yes, most inquisitive one. These are not ordinary water balloons," he said, holding one aloft. "These are filled with holy water."

"Holy water? Like from a church? How did you get holy water? Why did you get holy water?"

"You've never seen what holy water does to one of those blood suckers have you? It's deadly to them. You hit one of those creeps square with one of these," he said, as he threw one. He hit a tackling dummy with it, exploding the water all over it. "And he will dissolve in a matter of seconds. It's a great sight to see."

Wow, I thought. That must look so cool. Again—wait. Really? But I was now under his spell. I had to know more.

"How many vampires have you killed?" I asked excitedly.

"In terms of real numbers?" he asked.

"Yeah, how many?"

"Well . . . none, actually." He hung his head.

"What!" I yelled. "You're trying to put me in the middle of a bunch of real vampires and you've never killed one? Have you ever even seen one?"

I couldn't believe what an idiot I'd been. Here was a crazy person telling me all these things. Painting all these mental pictures of dissolving vampires and he'd never seen it?

I got up to leave.

"No—don't go!" he shouted, then continued in a normal volume. "It's all true—everything is true. The vampires are here—in the State Building. Everything I told you about my family really happened. My dad was working on this before his company sent him to Russia. I got his notes and started investigating on my own. The vampires are here, and that Stefan guy is after your mom." He reached into his backpack. "Here, look at these. I printed them from my Dad's computer." He threw some papers on the ground at my feet.

I knew I should leave, but what if . . . what if this was all real?

So, I forced myself to sit back down and look at his dad's stuff.

The papers he threw at me were his dad's notes on the old State Building. I sat back down on the grass and looked at them all. His father had been doing a lot of research on the night school and the vampires who ran it. There was a complete floor plan of the building (that might come in handy) and a semi-rundown on Stefan himself.

Stefan, it seems from what Stinky's father could tell, was at least two hundred fifty years old. Mr. Van Helsing had traced him back to Eastern Europe, then to France, then to London, and then here to Centerville. My question? Paris, London, Northern California? That doesn't make a lot of sense. How did he get here?

Well, the papers seemed to answer most of the questions. It seems there's a whole lot of vampires in Boston and New Orleans mostly. Stefan didn't want to be part of those families because he couldn't be in charge in those places, so he stopped in on New Orleans first, recruited a few vampires to come with him, and ended up here, where he made a few more.

I guess Mr. Van Helsing had vampire friends in New Orleans or something. There were letters from there to him, in all this fancy handwriting, warning him about what a jerk face Stefan was.

The part I didn't like is how they kept using the word, "dangerous." I really did have to get Mom away from him.

The papers were scary and amazing. Stinky could have saved a lot of time if he had shown me these before.

"You sure you don't want to wait for your dad?" I asked. "He obviously knows what's going on."

"There's no time. Right before he left, he told me to keep an eye on the building for him. That's why I was hiding in the bushes, not up in a tree where everybody could see me—like some people I know." He smiled at me. "Right after he left, the vampires started going out after night school let out and not coming back until right before dawn."

Stinky said he Zoomed with his dad in Russia and told him.

"They haven't done that before?" I asked him.

"Dad said they do occasionally, but if they're doing it all the time, it's not good. He told me to stay away."

"Why?"

"He said when they start going out frequently in public it means they've either run out of blood or they're looking for new members. Not a good thing in either case."

"Wow," I said. The more I heard, the more I didn't like.

"I figure they get enough blood from their drive, so it must be for more converts. So, I ignored my dad and followed one anyway."

"Isn't that dangerous? Can't they tell when they're being followed? Don't they have special powers at night?"

"Hey, they may be real old, and they may be real strong, and they may suck out the blood of humans, but they don't have eyes in the back of their heads. They're pretty easy to follow if you're careful."

"So, where did they go?" I asked.

"That's how I found out about you. I followed the guy called Leopold for two nights. Both nights he went to your house."

My world started spinning. Slowly at first, but it was picking up speed, fast. I staggered to my feet.

"Wait a minute," I yelled. "My house? Into my house?" I was standing right over him, yelling.

He jumped up and grabbed me by my shoulders.

"Calm down. Calm down. No, not into your house, just around it, kinda checking it out. I wanted to know who lived there, so I came back during the day and saw your family come out. I recognized you from school and your mom as a night school student. I put two and two together and figured they must be after your mom. Then I saw you in the tree. That's when I contacted you."

He looked at me, let go of me, and then lay back on the grass like it was all nothing. I was still standing right over him. It wasn't nothing.

"Why didn't you tell me this before? Why did you wait a week to tell me this?" I was really mad at him now. "Vampires at my house and you don't tell me? Why?" I was so angry I was trembling.

He looked up at me and shook his head. "I didn't know you well enough. How could I trust you? You would have told your mom and she would have told Stefan. Then he would know about me, and I would be toast. Dead toast. Dead, bloodless, toast."

I stood there, my mind racing again. This was too much brain activity for me. Every time I was sure I was going to get out of there, he said something sane.

"Okay. That actually makes sense. So, why tell me now?" I sat down on the grass next to him.

"I trust you. I like you. I want to help you. And because you can help me destroy them, which is what my family does." He reached down, picked up the gun thing, and started waving it around.

"Whoa . . . wait a minute. I told you I'm gonna help you, so put that thing away. I know enough about vampires to know bullets can't hurt them. Guns are nothing but bad for everyone around them. Get rid of the gun and I'll do anything you say." I hate guns.

"I wouldn't have a real gun, you idiot. They're too dangerous," he said. "This is an air gun. It shoots wood pellets by CO2 cartridges. Small sharp wooden pellets, kind of like mini-stakes, for shooting into their hearts."

"I remember the wooden sticks in the heart from the movies. Does it work? For real?"

He turned quickly, pointed the gun at the tackling dummy and fired. The gun made a hiss and pop.

"Did you hit it?" I jumped up and ran over to find out. There in the middle of the padding was a small hole with a splinter of wood barely sticking out.

"It works, all right," he said. "But it's never been used on a live target, so I don't know if it will work like a stake through the heart."

That started me thinking about what he was really saying. This time my brain stopped me. "Hold on, girl," my brain said to me. "Kill people? No way!" I realized right there I couldn't do it. I couldn't be part of this.

I walked back to him. This time I was the one who was calm.

"I know you have this all worked out," I said, "but you're talking about killing people, aren't you? Really killing people. Not a game. For real. And I. Can't. Kill. People. Why would you think I could? Why would you think you could? It's not right. You know it. It's also not legal." I was pointing my finger right at his face. Maybe I wasn't as calm as I thought.

"They're not people!" he shouted, standing up. "And they're not alive either. They're undead. What Stefan does when he converts them into vampires is worse than killing them. They have no control over their lives. Honest. They're not who they were at all, only undead shadows of themselves. Listen to me—he kills who they were. So, it wouldn't be us killing them. We'd be freeing them. Plus, they're like, really evil. It helps to know that."

Crap. He was making sense again.

He didn't stop. He was revved up now. "He controls them completely. They can't see themselves in the mirror or go out in the daylight or live the way they want. They're Stefan's servants. Hey, they exist on human blood. That's not my idea of living."

"So, they're kinda already dead?" Sometimes, maybe always, when talking to people about creatures you thought were fictional and found out weren't, you need complete clarity.

"My dad says they're completely already dead. We just let them rest in peace. Don't you understand? If he bites your mom three times, there's no coming back. You've lost her forever. Forever."

Everything just closed in on me at that moment. My poor brain was now tumbling around in my head. It might never recover. My clothes felt too tight, and I started pulling at them. My ponytail felt like it weighed a thousand pounds. I pulled my hair out of the ponytail and shook it around. I swear, if anyone had been watching from the street it would have looked like I was dancing up a storm and I can't dance. Stinky just watched me. Mouth open.

I finally calmed down. As I stood there in front of him, he was staring at me. My eyes narrowed "What are you looking at?"

"I . . . uh . . . you're really a girl."

"What? You didn't know that before?"

"I did. I knew. But . . . you're . . . pretty?"

It was then it occurred to me that Stinky was one of those boys who, faced with talking to a real girl, didn't know how. Until last year, it didn't matter. We all talked and joked, boys and girls. But then, well, things changed. I changed, too. And then some boys said some weird stuff that I ignored, some stared at you, and some stopped talking to girls altogether. Stinky was in the third category.

Mom had said it would happen. It sure did.

Standing there, my hair all wild around my face, I took a good look at Stinky. If he lost a few pounds, he might be cute . . .

Wait! A few seconds ago, we were talking about my mom being turned into a vampire and now our relationship has changed? No way. I gathered my hair, then searched the ground for my scrunchie.

"Looking for this?"

I looked up and Stinky was holding it out to me. I snatched it from his hand. "Thanks."

In no time the ponytail was back. But I don't think he looked at me the same way afterwards.

"I'm sorry," he said. "I never really—"

"Cut it out," I broke in before he could say more. "We're friends. Don't think of me as a girl, just as your partner."

He grinned. "I like that." He held his hand out to shake. It was kinda cute. We shook hands. He was instantly back in action mode.

"If we destroy Stefan now, he never gets his fangs into her," he said.

"I still have to wrap my head around this whole destroy thing." I was being honest with him.

He dropped to his knees. "Please help me. I told you. They're not people. You won't be killing people. You'll be saving people. Look, Jess—if we don't do this, you'll need a new mom."

The thought of losing my mom forever sent chills through my body. Mom . . . I started daydreaming about all the times she had covered for me when I did stupid things, all the times she was there when I needed to talk about anything, good or bad . . . everything about her. I love my mom. I couldn't lose her.

"Jess, are you okay?" Stinky interrupted my dream.

I felt my jaw clench. "We have to protect my mom," I told him.

"We can," he said. "And we can wipe out those bloodsucking

creeps at the same time."

We sat back down on the lawn, and he started my vampire hunting lessons. We must have talked for another two hours before I had to go home. He told me everything he knew. Everything his dad had told him about vampires.

By the time he was done, my brain felt like my stomach does on macaroni-and-cheese night at home: too full.

Before we left each other, he told me I had to vampire-proof the house and he explained how, with the garlic powder.

That night before I went to bed, I sneaked into the kitchen while Mom and Dad were watching TV and found the garlic powder. I went outside and sprinkled some on every window and around all the doors. Those guys weren't getting into my house.

March 10.

I finally got a look at Mom's neck. She had her hair pulled back. No bite marks. So far so good.

I re-garlicked the house just in case.

March 11.

Tuesday night. School night. I couldn't go and keep an eye on Mom because Dad caught me sneaking out to do just that. He asked a lot of questions. Good thing it was garbage night. I told him I was just going to take the bins out. He bought it. I think. Maybe. For sure, it surprised him. It drove me crazy, because not only did I have to take the garbage out, but I couldn't go watch Mom.

The worst part? Now he's going to expect me to remember to take the garbage out on my own from now on.

I called Stinky. He couldn't go out either. His mom was making him take a shower; then she had to cut his hair.

So, I decided to wait up for Mom, which Stinky thought was a great idea. While I waited, Half-Whit and I got in some real quality time together. He ignored me with his nose inside my garlic shoe and I pretended he wasn't farting.

Then finally, Mom got home.

He'd gotten her.

I didn't even have to look that hard. That ugly, skinny, cold, bloodsucking piece of garbage got her. The bite marks were clear on her neck.

Then, I couldn't help myself. I asked her about them.

She touched the bite marks with her fingertips and kinda smiled to herself, like I wasn't there asking her about them. Then she looked straight into my eyes and lied to me. My mom, who thinks lies are like the very worst thing any human can do, lied to me.

Mom said they were scratches from a tree branch she didn't see and had walked into. It was a nice try, but I knew. I couldn't tell her I knew, but I almost did. I almost slipped up.

"That doesn't look like any tree scratch I've ever seen" I said. She looked at me, thinking, not good, and I caught myself. "But what do I know about trees?"

Then I changed the subject.

I told her I'd be happy to put some medicine on the scratches for her. She put her hand over them again and said she would take care of it herself, and she stared at me in a strange way, for just a moment. It scared me. Mom had never scared me before.

She touched the bites again, got blood on her fingers, looked at it for a second, and then sucked it off! All while looking right at me like it was as natural as anything. Which, under circumstances like not being bitten by a vampire, it might be. Maybe. But ewwwwww.

Then, she walked away. Didn't say goodnight or tell me to brush my teeth or anything. This is serious.

Plus, I've never been so angry in my life. I wished Stefan was dead now. I wasn't going to have a problem killing. Not anymore.

But I wished I could tell Dad.

I did need to tell someone, so against any rational thought, I lifted Half-Whit onto the bed and told him. I think he actually listened before he fell over and went to sleep.

Now he thinks being on the bed is okay. Not a good night.

Half-Whit snored next to me, but I couldn't sleep. It was time for some action. Starting now.

March 12.

Okay, starting Saturday. Dad said I still couldn't go out on school nights.

At school on Friday, I met Stinky for lunch. He said I could get my supply of holy water that weekend. When I asked him how, he told me to fill up a bunch of water balloons, get my dog, and meet him at a big downtown church. The one on Central, near Tennyson. And that's all he would tell me.

I could maybe understand the balloons, but why Half-Whit?

Also today, I ducked a Rocco attack without knowing it. I guess he was waiting around a corner for me—at least that's what the kids said in math class—so I changed directions and didn't go that way. They said he punched the wall instead.

The wall lost.

I lucked out. I can't do that forever. I needed to figure something out. I needed to find some Rocco repellent. It's hard enough fighting vampires without having to fight the school bully, too.

March 15.

Even though I thought it was too early for anyone to see, Dad caught me making the water balloons in my bathroom. He just watched me for a moment and then asked, "Those for anything here? Because if you have thoughts of using them on Lily, think again."

I said, "No, no. It's for a big water balloon fight at the park—for charity."

He looked at me sideways and laughed. "Be careful and take a change of clothes. Have fun."

Sometimes I forget he was a kid once.

But I had lied to him again. I hate that. And it was getting easier. That's not good. But in my head, I make it okay for myself by saying it's to save Mom.

I left a while later carrying a large shopping bag full of water balloons and walking my disgusting Corgi. It wasn't going to be easy. I would only do this for Mom.

It's a long walk downtown. It's even longer when you're dragging a big lump of dog. I really believe people stared at us the whole way. About halfway there, Half-Whit stopped and refused to go any farther. I had a feeling something like this might happen, so I brought a few hot dogs with me. I told Half-Whit I would feed him if he would just walk into town with me. He must've understood because he started walking again, but only for a half a block at a time. He'd walk only that far, plop himself down and wait for a piece of hot dog, then get up and walk another half block and plop down again. It took us twice as long as usual to get there. I hate that dog.

When we finally got there, the front lawn of the church was crowded with what looked like hundreds of people and their pets. Dogs, cats, snakes, birds, pigs—you name it, they were there. Somehow, I found Stinky.

"What's going on here?" I asked. I don't think he heard me through all the barking and chirping and screeching. He held his hand up to his ear. "What's going on here?" I repeated but this time, I screamed it.

He motioned me away from all the animal noise. "Twice a year, the priests come out onto the lawn and bless all the animals. So, all we've got to do is put your water balloons in this saddlebag I got, strap it to your dog, and when they bless him, they bless the water balloons, and we've got holy water. Easy, huh?"

I pointed to my dog, my polish sausage with legs and said,

"You're going to put saddlebags on that?" Half-Whit kind of semi-partway looked at me, and I swear he rolled his eyes.

"Wow," Stinky said, finally taking a good look at Half-Whit. "I thought you said you had a real dog. What is that?"

Half-Whit sniffed at Stinky's shoe. Garlic. His tail wagged. Uh-oh. I think he was getting sleepy. Or falling in love.

"Hey, he's a real dog and he might just qualify as a pet for this thing." I moved Half-Whit away from Stinky's shoes. "There's no test or anything is there?" Half-Whit, already under a shoe-induced garlic trance, had rolled over on his side and had one leg in the air.

Stinky sighed. "Nope. It just has to be someone's pet." Then he pointed down at Half-Whit. "It looks like you're going to have to hold him in your arms and drape the saddlebags over him."

"Hold him?" I said. "I can't even stand to look at him."

Half-Whit was now on his back, four legs in the air and sound asleep. Somehow, he had wormed his way down the sidewalk on his back and had his nose right on Stinky's shoe. As I kept telling myself, I was doing this for my mom. I bent down and picked up my dog. It was like picking up a giant boneless chicken.

I carried him over and got in the line with what seemed like every other animal in town.

There I stood, a totally limp sleeping dog covered with saddlebags full of water balloons nestled in my arms, waiting to be blessed. It wasn't very long until my arms fell asleep and I finally had to put him down. He just slept. It seemed like hours before the priests got to us. I'm surprised they even came near us, actually. Half-Whit looked like someone threw up a dog.

As they got closer, the older priest said to me, "My, my, young lady—what kind of unusual animal is this?" He pointed down at Half-Whit.

"I know it doesn't look like it, but it's a dog."

The priest looked kind of shocked. Half-Whit looked kind of dead.

"What's that on his back?" the other priest asked.

I couldn't tell them about the water balloons. There was a long pause. Too long.

"That dog is very sick," Stinky came out of nowhere to say. "He can hardly walk." Stinky pointed to the saddlebags. "And that's his back brace."

"Oh, my," said the older priest. "We must doubly bless this poor creature." They spent extra time doing it, too. One of them even got on his knees. When they were done, I knew we had the holy water we needed.

But Stinky wasn't done yet. He pulled up a red wagon with a twenty-gallon fish tank on it. "Father, could you bless my goldfish?" he said. It was brilliant. There was one little goldfish in that great big tank. An instant twenty gallons of holy water ready for us to use.

We really must've looked dorky going home though. Me carrying that sleeping dog with all those water balloons strapped to him and Stinky pulling that little red wagon with twenty gallons of holy water in it. He had to pull it carefully because we couldn't afford to waste a drop.

Halfway home, we had to feed the goldfish to Half-Whit, so he would let me keep on carrying him.

Once I was home, I hid the water balloons in the garage refrigerator so they wouldn't shrink. That was Stinky's idea. He's kind of a water balloon expert. I put them behind a bunch of cans of vegetable juice. No one will ever find them there. I think that juice is like ten years old.

Then Half-Whit and I went into the house. Mom caught us coming in. I froze, hoping she wouldn't ask where we had been. Instead, she said she was happy I was taking more interest in my dog. She said it would make Grandma happy to know how close Whitman and I had gotten.

I smiled and said, "Thanks, Mom. We were closer than ever today."

I hope I never have to get that close to him again.

Then it occurred to me that Mom was acting kind of normal, thinking about her mother and the dog and me. I felt a little better. Maybe she's okay.

March 16.

I was wrong. Family day. No Mom. Let me repeat myself. Family. Day. No. Mom. This happens . . . never. Where was she? Turned out she was at the library doing schoolwork. Stinky said he thought Stefan was making her leave the house so she gets used to being without us, away from her family. Especially on a family day.

If that undead guy thought he was going to do that, he had

another think coming. No way. I had to think of something.

I went to find Dad. He was in the backyard watering the plants. Lily was helping him. They were laughing and making a game out of it. I watched for moment. How could I make him understand? Then I got the best idea ever. At least for right then.

I told Dad we should go to the library and surprise Mom. We could take her out to lunch or out for some ice cream or something. Make it a family day after all. Lily thought it was great idea and started yelling, "Ice cream!"

Dad thought it was a great idea, too, and said I was a good daughter to be thinking of my mom. If he'd only known.

We went to the library. I was feeling pretty good about myself. This was a great plan. Except we couldn't find her. As we looked through all the rows of books, I could see Dad was getting more and more serious.

Once we were sure she wasn't there and Dad was trying not to show how upset he was getting, I had a thought. Not a good thought but a thought. The State building is just a block from the library. Stinky said Stefan would have power over Mom once he bit her. Not completely, but enough. Maybe enough to have her go to him? Worth a shot.

So I said to Dad, "Maybe she got her book and is reading outside. It's a nice day. Maybe she's over by the State Building. They have nice benches. It's close."

Now, I know the park across the street is prettier and has better places to sit, but somehow, I knew she'd be at the State Building.

Dad calmed down a little and tugged my ponytail gently. “Good thought, kiddo,” he said.

We found her on a bench in front of the State Building. I hate being right when it’s stuff like this.

I saw her first. She was sitting, her book closed on her lap, staring at the building. I ran full speed, yelling, “Mom! Mom!”

She sprang up like we’d caught her toilet papering somebody’s house, not that I’d know anything about that personally. That my parents know.

I ran right up to her, smiling. It might have been a half fake smile because of why she was there. If she noticed, she didn’t let on.

“What’s going on?” she asked, kinda flustered. Then Dad and Lily got there.

“Family day!” I said. “We came to get you.”

Then she did something that made the hair on the back of my neck stand straight up. She snuck a look back at the building before looking back at us. Only I noticed it.

I grabbed her hand. “Let’s get out of here and get some—”

“ICE CREAM!!” Lily screamed.

Mom looked at us all and smiled. “Good idea,” she said.

She spent family day with us after all. This was a win. There was no way I was going to let that bloodsucker outwit me. Even if he was two hundred thirty-six years older.

March 17.

Stinky and me had lunch together at school. When I told him

what happened, he shook his head. "It's worse than I thought," he said.

"Why?"

"Staring at the building? She's got it bad. You've gotta stop her from going to school tomorrow night."

"He can't bite her again yet, can he? That's what you said."

"No, he can't. At least I don't think he can, but he can exert his power over her. That's something we can't afford. Just stop her from going."

And that's what I'm going to do.

March 18.

Hip, hip hooray! Mom didn't go to class. It wasn't me. It wasn't Dad. It was all thanks to Lily. Bless her heart. That sweet little girl came down with a world class case of chicken pox.

The pre-school called Mom in the afternoon and told her to come and get Lily. When Mom got her home, Lily looked like a puffed-up Dalmatian. I'd never seen so many spots, and so fast. There was a chicken pox outbreak at her school. When I had the chicken pox, I had maybe three or four spots. I guess Lily got hers, plus all the ones I didn't get, too.

That night, I could tell Mom really wanted to go to night school. She kept saying she couldn't afford to miss a class, that it was important. I figured it was Stefan's control that was affecting her. She was struggling with herself. I could see it. It was scary. Stefan was calling to her, but she also needed to be with her sick baby.

We won. Lily won. Mom won. She beat Stefan. She stayed home. I guess one bite isn't stronger than genuine mother-type feelings. That's a good thing to know. I just had to keep her from being bitten again. Stinky and me were going to start working on that this weekend.

March 20.

Over sandwiches (mine was normal, his looked like a sea creature that was still alive), Stinky and I got it all worked out. He would tell his mom he was going to the movies with me Saturday night. He said his mom would let him go on a spaceship to Mars if it was with a real girl.

I would tell my parents I was going to the movies with Danielle, then to her house for a sleepover. Yeah, another lie. Mom and Dad didn't know Stinky even existed. He wanted it that way so there'd be an "element of surprise" later on. I'm not sure what he meant by that, but he hadn't been wrong yet. So that was the plan. That way we could go out and do what we had to do.

Plus, they would never let me go out with a boy alone—not yet, anyways. Not even somebody like Stinky. No way. Dad always told me he had a written test, and that any boy who wanted to date me would have to wait until I was nineteen or something. I knew he was kidding. I hope he was kidding.

So, I had all my stuff together in the garage, ready for Saturday. Only one problem—I needed my own stash of garlic powder. I went to the kitchen to get some but couldn't find it. Mom caught me going through the cupboard and wanted to know what I was doing. I told her I wanted to make some garlic bread but couldn't find the garlic.

"Oh, I'm sorry, baby," said Mom. "I threw out the garlic salt yesterday. It smelled like it had spoiled." Yeah, right—like garlic salt can spoil. She just couldn't stand the smell. She's changing.

So, I started a list of stuff I needed to buy. Garlic powder was on the top. Okay, it was the only thing on the list. But knowing Stinky, there would be more soon.

March 21.

I tried to talk to Mom after school. I told you before—she has always made time for me no matter what she has going on. Well, before the bites on her neck.

Mom is always the first one to volunteer to help at my school. At Lily's school, too. Last year my school gave her an award for all the help she gave them.

"I don't need a reward for doing the things I love to do," she said at the ceremony in front of the whole school. "I've gotten more back from all of you than I could ever give."

Even the teachers stood and clapped. It was great having all my friends think my mom was so cool.

A couple of years ago, Molly Harris told me she wanted my mom to be her mom. Molly said it was because my mom wasn't mean or anything. Then she came up close and whispered to me, asking if Mom was mean when no one else could see. I told her no, she's the same everywhere. She said, "Lucky," and walked away.

But this day as I tried to talk to Mom, I could see more changes in her. Not so lucky. But I still tried.

"Hey, Mom," I yelled as I came through the front door. "I'm home and I've got good news."

Usually, this kind of greeting would get me a smile and a hug and maybe even an offer of some ice cream and, at the very least, interest in what my news was. This time she barely looked up from her art book.

"That's nice, honey," she said, nose going back into the book.

"Don't you want to know what it is?"

It took her a moment, but she put her book down. "Sure, sweetheart. What is it?"

"Mrs. Foster wants to know if you'll work at the carnival again this year. I told her you'd probably love to. She said the booth you did last year made more money for the science department than any ever."

Mrs. Foster was my science teacher and had loved Mom's pie booth. I think she bought and ate most of them herself. She looks like she's eaten a lot of pies.

"I'll even help you make the pies," I said.

"I'm sorry, honey," Mom said. "But with night school and everything, I don't think I have the time. So please don't volunteer me for anything right now, okay?"

Crap.

This is not my mom. I wanted to cry.

March 22.

Saturday. The time to act had finally come.

About five-thirty, I told Mom and Dad I was going to Danielle's. Dad asked me to leave her number and when I'd be home. Like a dad. Mom didn't even tell me to have a good time.

I took half a dozen water balloons from the garage fridge, the last of the garlic powder Stinky had given me, a sleeping bag, and my backpack. Yes, I knew I still needed to buy my own garlic.

Stinky met me at the park across the street from the old State Building. He had his backpack, a couple of flashlights, some water balloons, and the pellet gun. I told him to only pull it out in an emergency.

We set ourselves up in the bushes across the street from the night school. The plan was to follow any of the vampires who came out. Since there was no night school on Saturday, we figured they'd come out early. We wanted to see what they were up to. I wanted to see if they went back to my house.

Except we were wrong about the early part. No one came out for hours and it was getting cold. I had to walk around to keep warm. Stinky kept telling me to get down. Finally, I'd had enough and got up to leave.

I took two steps and Stinky swung his legs around, knocking mine out from under me. I went down with a crash in the bushes. Before I could yell, Stinky had his hand over my mouth.

"Shut up and look," he said, pointing toward the State Building.

"Errrgggererggg," I said. Stinky still had his hand over my mouth. I had to bite it.

"Ow! Why'd you do that?" he whispered loudly.

"I couldn't breathe, you idiot." I evil-eyed Stinky there in the bushes. "Why'd you knock me down?" I asked.

"Shut up and look." He was pointing across the street.

I got on my hands and knees and looked. Stefan was standing on the front steps with two men. I couldn't hear what they were saying, but Stefan was doing most of the talking. You could tell because he was moving his cold boney hands all over the place and pointing down the street toward the center of town. One of the men shook his hand and started walking away. Stefan and the other one stayed. I watched them as they started talking to each other.

Suddenly, the first man crossed the street and headed straight at us. We froze. He got within about ten feet of us, then turned up the sidewalk and went on down the street. He hadn't seen us.

What a great pair of vampire hunters we were. I was so scared I couldn't move. I didn't get out the garlic or holy water or anything. He could have come, grabbed us both, sucked out all our blood, and we'd probably still be frozen in fear in the bushes. Dead, with no blood, and still frozen with fear. What a couple of dorks.

As soon as we were sure he was gone, Stinky whispered, "I got a good look at him. Did you?"

He could have been a spider monkey for all I knew. I had just seen my life pass before my eyes, not someone's face. "You've got to be kidding," I whispered back.

"Well, I'd know him for sure if I saw him again," he said

proudly.

"I for one don't care if I ever see him again, because—" Stinky put his hand over my mouth again. I bit him again. "Cut that out," I said.

He just shook his hand and whispered, "There goes another one. We'll follow him."

The other vampire who had been talking to Stefan was headed downtown on the other side of the street. I looked back at the old State Building. Stefan was gone. I turned back to tell Stinky, but he was gone, too. He had taken off to track the vampire. I grabbed my balloon bag and garlic and ran after him.

I saw Stinky sneaking down the sidewalk about half a block behind the second vampire, on the opposite side of the street. Once in a while Stinky would disappear behind a tree, then pop out again, all the time keeping an eye on the vampire. It was kind of fun watching him.

It was then I realized I was standing out in the open watching all of this. If the guy Stinky was following turned around, he would see me for sure. I jumped back in the bushes. After a while, when my heart stopped beating so fast, I peeked out and couldn't see Stinky or the vampire.

I couldn't stay in those bushes forever, even though that sounded like a pretty good idea right then.

Carefully, I snuck from tree to tree down the street. I finally got to the corner. The streetlight on my side of the street was out, but the one on the other side was bright. Only a couple of cars had come down the street in the last few minutes. It was after midnight now for sure. Oh yeah. New day.

March 23.

It was cold, it was dark, and I was all alone on that sidewalk. I thought about just going home, but I couldn't leave Stinky by himself. He was depending on me.

But first, I had to find him. I took a deep breath and dashed across the street. I jumped into the first bush I saw. As I was about to sneak further down the block, a hand reached out and grabbed me from behind. I screamed. Well, I tried to scream, but I was so startled nothing came out. I think I squeaked.

Behind me a voice said, "He went into the alley behind the rat hole." It was Stinky. I had it all figured out now. Vampires wouldn't have to kill me—Stinky would just scare me to death. I wanted to punch him out. Then I realized what he said.

"The vampire went into a rat hole?" I asked. Hey, why not, I thought to myself. Maybe they can't be bats, but maybe they can be rats. That made as much sense as anything else I'd seen and heard lately.

"No, you dweeb, the Rat Hole. You know what that is. Wake up," Stinky said in a way that made me want to slap him. Then, a light bulb went off in my head. Wait. It didn't go off, it went on. Grrrrr. This night was making me crazy. But I did know what he was talking about.

It was the Rat Hole. The pool hall and bar on 2nd street. My dad took me there to teach me to play pool once, a couple of years ago. It was a great place. Sawdust on the floor, lots of pool tables, free peanuts—and you could throw the shells on the floor and not even get in trouble. And there were lots of really weird people to watch . . .

They wouldn't let me sit at the cool, carved wooden bar to drink my ginger ale because of the law or something, but otherwise, it was awesome. Plus, they had French fries with gravy and cheese on them. It was perfect.

Except Mom went crazy when she found out Dad had taken me there. I wanted to go back as soon as possible. Mom said something about pigs flying. Dad never took me back.

"He went into a pool hall?" I asked. "Do vampires like to play pool?" A very good question, I thought, that may never be answered.

"No, he went down the alley behind it," said Stinky. "I'm going to check it out." He walked a few steps and turned around. "You coming or what?"

I guess I was because I did. We stashed everything but two balloons each in the bushes and headed for the Rat Hole.

There we were, two junior high school kids, sneaking around a pool hall in the middle of the night looking for vampires. Just as we walked by the front door, it swung open and a man stumbled out. Stinky jumped back about ten feet.

"It's the other one!" he screamed. "DIE!" He threw a water balloon and hit the man directly in the face. And nothing happened. So, he threw his other balloon. Direct hit. Nothing again, except that the man was very mad and very wet.

"Hey, you kids!" the man yelled. "What do you think you're

doing? I don't know who you punks think you are, but I'm calling the police." He pointed directly at me and pulled out his wet cell phone. That was enough for me. I took off down the street. "Come back here, you punks!" the man yelled. I looked back to see him go back into the Rat Hole, and I saw Stinky run around the corner and into the alley instead of following me.

I ran a few more steps and then stopped. "I don't believe this," I said to myself, out loud. Nobody in sight. No cars on the street. And Stinky fearlessly went after that other vampire. With no balloons.

My thoughts? I gotta go and get Stinky. I can't leave him there alone. I closed my eyes, took a deep breath again, and ran back toward the alley.

I stopped at the edge of the building and looked around the corner, down the alley. It was a short alley, maybe a little less than a full block long, with solid brick buildings down both sides. It dead-ended at the back of another brick building. The alley was lined on both sides with maybe half a dozen big metal dumpsters for the businesses in the area to put their garbage into. It also didn't smell very good.

There were only two lights in the whole alley, one on the side door of the pool hall building, and one on the door on the opposite side, and they were dim. It took me a minute to get used to the light, but I still couldn't see everything down the alley because of the shadows.

As far as I could tell, there was nobody in sight—no Stinky, no vampire, and plenty of places to hide, so I had to be careful. I got low and crept down the left side of the alley.

Staying low, I worked my way down to the end of the alley. The darkness made it hard to see anything at all. The further I went, the worse it smelled. Plus, I had to be careful not to break my water balloons. Vampire hunting is complicated. There's a lot to think about.

"Stinky, where are you?" I said softly. "Come on—let's get out of here." It was still quiet. I looked back down the alley toward the street. "Stinky, let's go. Don't do this to me. The police will be here any minute. That bloodsucker is still around here somewhere, too."

As soon as I said that, the second vampire's silhouette appeared in the middle of the alley, his back to the street, red eyes glowing, looking right at me. I was trapped.

As he stepped into the dim light, I saw he was holding Stinky off the ground by the back of his neck. "Is this what you're looking for?" he asked. Stinky was making a gurgling noise.

"Stop it," I said. "Please don't hurt him. Put him down and I'll come out." I had no choice. The vampire dropped him in a heap. He looked down at Stinky. "Move and you die." He was so calm the way he said it, I knew he meant it and it made me more scared than I have ever been in my whole life. Okay, I know I say that a lot, but every time I got scared it got worse. Honest. My whole life. Which, the way it was looking, might end tonight.

I walked out into the alley. Stinky gasped for breath and stayed on the ground. The vampire jumped back, grabbed a dumpster with one hand and, with no effort at all, slid it out to block the entrance to the alley. It didn't look real. Nobody is that strong.

"Now come here," he said. I slipped one of the water balloons behind my back under my shirt and walked further out, into the light. Stinky was still on the ground, but he was breathing normally now.

The vampire looked me over. "Okay, sweetheart—"

I'm going to stop right now and say that was the moment I went from scared to mad. Mom said when strangers call you things like that, they're underestimating you. "Don't let anybody underestimate you, even if it's a vampire," she told me. Okay, she didn't say the vampire part, but right then, that's what I heard in my head.

"Whatever that is in your hand, drop it now," the vampire said to me, his eyes still glowing red. I dropped the balloon, gently. It didn't break. It just sat there on the ground.

"Who are you and how do you know about me and what I am? Your friend wouldn't tell me anything. He's lucky you came when you did."

"Let him go and I'll tell you everything." I had to stall for time. Maybe the first guy had really called the police. But then why would a vampire say he's gonna call the police? My brain was kinda hurting again because it was working so much.

The vampire kicked at Stinky. "Get up," he ordered. Stinky slowly got up and looked straight at me, then down at the unbroken water balloon at my feet, then back at me. Then he slowly stuck his hands into his pockets and winked at me.

Oh no. What's going on?

"I need an answer, now. How do you know about me?"And then the vampire growled at me.

Now Stinky had a big grin on his face. He winked again. Another light bulb. Stinky is a genius.

"Come and get it, red eyes," I answered. I had nothing to lose anyways.

"I'm growing tired of this," the vampire said. As he started toward me, he grabbed Stinky tightly by the shirt and pulled him along. Stinky still had his hands in his pockets. I backed up. The balloon sat untouched on the ground a few feet in front of me. Stinky looked down at the balloon and then at me.

"Come on, you undead dork," I said. My voice was shaking now, but I had to keep his attention on me.

He walked straight at me, keeping Stinky right beside him. As their feet got near the water balloon on the ground, Stinky lunged toward it, raised his foot, and with all his might, stomped it into the pavement. The balloon exploded with a whoosh and splashed water all over the vampire's feet and ankles.

Instantly, the vampire's feet and legs started smoking. He let out a howl and started jumping up and down in pain. Stinky used that moment to pull away from him.

Just then, a police car showed up at the mouth of the alley, lights flashing. Only the dumpster kept them from driving in. The police turned the car spotlight down the alley, but the dumpster blocked that, too.

Stinky pulled his hands from his pockets. They were full of garlic powder. He threw it directly in the vampire's face, blinding him. “Now, Jess! NOW!” Stinky screamed.

I pulled the water balloon from behind my back and threw it at the vampire’s chest. He took a direct hit.

His whole body was smoking now. He went down to his knees for a second, raised his head, and looked at me with shock in his eyes, then fell straight down on the pavement. It took just a few seconds more for his whole body to turn to dust.

“Hold it right there, you kids,” a voice said. “This is the police.” We both put our hands up in the air. Another police car arrived at the alley entrance. It was looking like a cop convention now.

Two policemen came up and shined their flashlights in our faces. “Where’s the other one?” the first policeman asked. “I thought I counted three of you down here.” That’s when I realized they hadn’t seen anything that happened. They must have been getting out of the car and missed everything. They didn’t know!

Stinky must have realized this too because he said, “Oh no, sir, officer, sir, there’s just the two of us here.” All the time Stinky was talking, he was shuffling around, moving his feet like he had to go to the bathroom. But he didn’t have to go to the bathroom—he was kicking the vampire dust around. He didn’t want the police asking questions about a human shaped pile of dust lying in the middle of the alley.

“Stand still,” the policeman ordered. We both raised our hands higher.

And that’s how we ended up at the police station. We also

found out why the holy water didn't affect the first guy we hit. And why he called the police. He wasn't a vampire. He was the city director of recreation and had been at the old State Building for a meeting with Stefan. All throwing the water balloon at him had done was get him wet—and warn the real vampire that we were there. And, worst of all, get us taken to the police station.

We also found out the police guys were pretty cool. They laughed while they told us the recreation director wasn't going to press charges against me and Stinky because he didn't want his wife to know he was hanging around the Rat Hole. I guess his wife liked the place as much as Mom did.

All the policemen really wanted to know was how we moved that dumpster. They said it took a truck to move it back. I told them the truth. We didn't move it.

Well, we didn't.

It was four o'clock in the morning by the time my dad got to the police station to pick us up. And, needless to say, he was less than happy.

I had to explain why Stinky wasn't Danielle, and that wasn't good. Stinky had to tell Dad we were just friends, out having fun. With water balloons. After midnight. And Stinky, who keeps getting cooler all the time, also told Dad it was all his fault, that he talked me into it.

It was a very silent trip in the car. Dad kept sniffing like he was trying to smell something. Stinky was still kinda covered with the garlic power he'd thrown in the alley.

We dropped Stinky off at his house. As he walked to his front door, Dad looked at me. "He didn't try and kiss you or anything, did he?"

I laughed. "Did you smell him?" I said. "No. he didn't try and kiss me." The garlic was coming in handy in more than one way. "He's just a friend, Dad. Honest."

I made up a great story about how we met at school and had so much in common and there was no boyfriend/girlfriend thing at all and that he didn't have any other friends at school and a bunch of other junk. I almost overdid it until Dad held up his hand for me to stop, then didn't say anything else as we drove home.

In our driveway, Dad finally yelled at me. I think it was building up all the way home because it was epic. Dad doesn't yell at me very often. This time, he thought he had a good reason. I get it.

He couldn't understand what had gotten into to us that we'd be out in the middle of the night throwing water balloons at city officials. That we were real lucky to be let off with a warning. That it's dangerous out there.

He has no idea.

I hung my head and mumbled something about being totally sorry. I wanted to tell him everything, but he was so mad it would be stupid to try. But then, he'd never believe it if he wasn't mad, either. And that was the problem.

Dad told me to go to bed and that we would sort this all out in the morning. Then he looked at me in a way you never want your dad to look at you. "Wait. It is morning. I guess I need some coffee," and he walked off to the kitchen. It's gonna be a long day.

As I walked down the hall toward my room, I saw Mom peeking at me around the door of her bedroom. She didn't say a thing. I looked right at her. No emotion. No nothing. Then she closed the door.

Just when I think it can't get worse, I thought. The old mom would have been the first one out of the house to see if I was all right. Heck, she would have come with Dad and dragged Lily there. It was like she didn't care. I needed her to care. I need her for stuff like that. I started crying as I walked to my room.

Half-Whit was on my bed. He raised his head up when I came in and looked at me liked he understood, for a moment. Then he farted. I put him on the floor and lay down. I was really tired. I'd destroyed my first vampire and I guess that takes a lot out of you.

Lying there, my eyes open, I thought of one thing that really worried me. How long would it be before Stefan started looking for his vampire pal? And what would he do next? What would we do next? We couldn't keep following them and dusting them—they would figure that out fast. I don't think they're dumb. You can't live for over two hundred years without learning something. No, we would have to make other plans.

But not now, I thought. I have to get some sleep.

And I did. Then I had to face the day.

I was sure my dad was going to give me another hard time when I woke up after noon. I didn't know what I'd say this time because I'd used up all the made-up stories I had. Except Stinky and I are friends and I think I'm his only friend. So those weren't lies. Neither was the boyfriend/girlfriend thing.

Wow . . . I didn't lie after all.

I just left out the vaporized vampire.

I can't get caught again, though. Stinky had the bug thing to tell his mom. No such luck for me.

It also occurred to me that we would have to go back and get the rest of our stuff out of the bushes. All our water balloons (which I now knew worked) and Stinky's air gun were still out there, and we couldn't afford to lose them.

Mom and Dad didn't say too much to me after I left my room and went to face them. In fact, Mom didn't say anything. Dad just asked me a few more questions about Stinky and his family, and then he wanted to know what we were really doing out so late at night, now that I'd had time to think about telling him the truth. So I took a deep breath, and I told him we were out collecting bugs for Stinky's mom. I can't believe I used the bug thing.

When Dad stopped laughing, he said he now knew why I had flunked creative writing in summer school last year.

"I didn't flunk. I got a D," I said.

"Doesn't matter. You had all night to think of a better story than that." He laughed again. He also said he was going to call Stinky's mom and get to the bottom of this.

Thank goodness Stinky's family is so weird. Dad called the Van Helsings and Stinky's mom invited him over to see her bug collection. No kidding. It was great. Plus, she told Dad that she was delighted that I was interested in bugs, too.

Dad ended the call, rolled his eyes, shook his head, kinda

apologized, and said, “I can’t prove it, but I think you got away with something here. So be warned.”

He also said I shouldn’t be out so late again without supervision. So please don’t do it anymore. And no more bug collecting. And no more of whatever we were really doing. And finally—no more water balloons. Then he half smiled.

Yep, I thought. He was a kid once.

“I mean it about the water balloons,” he said. He was still smiling.

“I won’t throw them at any more living things, I promise,” I answered. I didn’t say I wouldn’t throw them at undead things.

Stinky called later that night. He told me he went out and got all the stuff from the bushes. It was all still there. That was good. Otherwise it would have meant another trip with Half-Whit to get him blessed. I didn’t think I could take that again. Neither could the priests.

March 25.

Mom was going back to night school tonight, so at school today I asked Stinky if it was soon enough for Stefan to bite her again. I know, I keep asking him the same question, but this one is important. He once again said he was sure it was too soon, that she couldn’t get bitten again for another two or three weeks. At least according to what his dad told him. Thank goodness. We had time.

Mom got home late again, and I had to keep pinching myself to stay awake to wait for her. Lying in bed, I could hear her telling Dad that one of the night school teachers quit and needed to be replaced.

That must have been the guy we dusted in the alley, I thought. But it was what she told him next that made me sit straight up in bed, almost knock Half-Whit onto the floor, and get chills up my back.

She told dad that Stefan would like her to consider teaching at the night school next semester.

OVER MY DEAD BODY.

March 26.

We had some kind of achievement test at school, the Idaho Potato Brain Test or something. You know, the kind with the multiple guess answers. LIKE:

"Johnny has $4.57. He wants to buy some apples. They cost 49 cents each. How long does it take for each train to reach New Jersey?

A. Cairo, Egypt
B. An apricot
C. A Rectangle
D. Both B and C"

Maybe the questions weren't quite that bad, but close, very close. I'm sure I did real well. Not.

Right after the test there was another Rocco sighting. Just what I needed. He jumped out from behind the corner of a building, his fists up to punch me into another dimension. "Time to pay up, Trueheart," he said, a huge grin on his face.

I pointed to his pants and said, "Your zipper's down."

He stopped mid-punch and looked down, and I ran away. I'll bet I did better on the test than he did.

Once again, I barely escaped with my life. I have to figure out a way to do something about Rocco. But after I save my mom.

Speaking of Mom, she was acting real weird again, and because of the tests, I didn't have a chance to talk to Stinky at school. So I called him from home.

As I wrote before in this diary, unlike a milliony billion of my friends, I do not own a cell phone. What you also don't know is that I don't have a TV in my bedroom. I do have a computer, but it's not the one connected to the Internet. That one is in the family room.

My parents say it's because they love me, they do these things. I used to think it was because we were poor, but after watching my friends get lost in their phones and talk about some of the stuff they look at on the Internet, I kinda get what they mean. Kinda.

So, we have real plug-into-the-wall phones, along with Mom's and Dad's cell phones. Phones from the Stone Age. That's what I get to use.

So, like I said, I called Stinky on the phone with a cord in the kitchen. No one else was in there. We started off talking about the achievement tests and how stupid they were, and I told him about how Rocco almost pounded me to China. Then Stinky changed the subject to something about the night school blood drive in the next couple of weeks.

"Could we do something to mess it up?" I asked. "You know, like starve them out?"

"Wait a minute," Stinky said. "I think I hear somebody else on this line. Is there somebody listening on your extension?"

"You're crazy," I answered. "Not even Lily is that stupid," Then it hit me. I closed my eyes and said into the phone, hoping I was wrong, "Mom? Mom, are you there? Is that you?" There's a phone extension next to Mom and Dad's bed.

It was Mom. I couldn't believe it.

"Oh, I'm sorry honey," she said, and her voice was cold—really cold. "I picked up the phone to make a call. Sorry if I interrupted you."

"Hi, Mrs. Scott," Stinky said. "It's Abraham. A friend of Jessica's from school."

Jessica? Grrrr.

"Abraham? That's an unusual name these days. What's your last name?"

There was a pause from Stinky's end. "Van Helsing," he finally said. "Nice to meet you." Stinky was trying to be polite, but we needed to talk about this Jessica thing.

Mom answered him. "Nice to meet you, too. Jess, honey, did I hear you talking about the night school blood drive? I'm supposed to work at the next one." Her voice was unusually flat. It didn't sound like her at all.

"Oh no, Mrs. Scott," Stinky said quickly. "You must have

heard me wrong. I said LUNCH LINES, not blood drive. I was complaining about the long lunch lines at school. I'm going to bring my lunch from now on." I don't know how he thinks so fast.

"Well, that's very nice," she said. "I'm sorry if I misunderstood you. I'll let you two go on talking." She hung up the extension.

"That was way too close," Stinky said. "We can't talk on your phone anymore. Your Mom'll start telling Stefan everything she hears from now on."

"Then why did you tell her your real name?" I asked.

"Because sometimes I'm not very smart, okay? I'm a kid." That excuse was lame and he knew it, but he knows it works a lot on grownups. Not on other kids though. "I'm counting on her not remembering it," he admitted.

"She's not really Mom anymore, is she?" I thought I was going to cry.

Stinky must have heard it in my voice because he said, "Cool out. She's still your mom, but Stefan is getting more control every day. Pull yourself together and meet me at lunch tomorrow. We gotta make more plans."

I went back to my room, kicked my shoes off, and lay down next to Half-Whit on the bed. Just as I made the mistake of thinking I would hug him for a little comfort, he jumped off the bed and put his nose in my shoe.

I had to figure out a way to palm him off on Lily.

March 27.

Stinky and I met at lunch. He had another one of those flyers the vampires printed up. It said the next blood drive was starting Thursday, on April 3rd. He figured the vampires would start putting up posters and signs for the blood drive on Sunday or Monday night.

"Let's tear all the signs down," I said. "Nobody sees them, nobody goes." I was thinking more like Stinky every day.

"I took all the flyers from the grocery store already," he bragged. "We could also call the newspaper and tell them the blood drive has been canceled."

"Yeah, and with no food available, they'll starve," I said back.

"Or come after us for a meal."

"Don't remind me," I said nervously. "But if we're careful, they'll never know it was us."

"That depends. Can you get out Sunday night?"

"I'll have to sneak out," I said. "I've never done that before. You're lucky. You have that bug collecting thing going for you. I have no excuse at all, and after last weekend I don't think my dad is going to be too thrilled about me going out. I don't think Mom'll care." Most kids would love that. It made me sad. I looked him in the eye. "But have no fear, I will get out."

"Be sure to garlic all the windows and doors before you leave. We can't have any surprises when you get home," he said.

I made a mental note not to forget to buy garlic. Again.

March 29.

Mom and Dad had an actual fight this morning. I heard it from my room. I can count on one hand the times I've heard them really fight. She was yelling at him. Stinky said a couple of days ago that Stefan would work on Mom to distance herself from the family so that when she left for good it would be okay for her psychologically. Listening to them, I agreed this had to be part of Stefan's plan.

Mom was yelling at Dad about wanting the sink in the bathroom replaced or something. Nothing she would ever have yelled at him about before. I needed to get in there and stop this.

I ran down the hall. Half-Whit waddled after me. I knocked on the door and Mom stopped yelling. I didn't wait for her to answer. I opened the door and stuck my head in.

"You okay?" I asked. "I thought I heard something."

I tried to act all innocent and stuff. Mom looked at me like I'd just set Lily on fire. All mean, like nothing I had seen before. It was silent for a moment, then Half-Whit squeezed past me and farted—loud. It smelled bad. Like really bad.

Instantly, the fight was over, as Dad went, "Oh, my Lord," and walked out holding his nose. Mom acted like she didn't smell it.

"You okay?" I said again, trying not to cough because of the cloud Half-Whit had produced.

"Never better," Mom answered. "Just have some things to do." Then she walked by me and out of the room. I looked down at my dog.

"That's one way to break up a fight. I'll give you that." Then I think he kinda winked at me and walked out and down the hall.

I spent the rest of the day working on my escape plan. To make it work, I volunteered to clean the screens on my bedroom windows. Dad was amazed, but happy to see me working around the house. It's a good thing they were so gross and dirty looking or maybe he would have figured out I was up to something. He didn't.

Mom stopped and watched me for a minute but didn't say anything. I don't like new Mom.

Anyways, it was a crummy job, but I kept telling myself I was using a scrub brush to save my mom's life. I figured I would put one of the screens back on with the screws loose, so when I wanted to leave, I would pull off the screen and out I'd go. Easy.

Not easy. I had a trial run. I forgot about the rose bushes under my windows. To top it off, Dad had just watered them. I got out and back in okay, but my shoes needed cleaning and my pants would have to be replaced.

I also used up the rest of my garlic powder doing the windows and doors. Mental note: Buy some more. And some Band-Aids.

March 30.

Sunday. Time to try the escape plan. I was ready, just had to wait for night.

The time passed quicker when Dad came in to tell me how proud he was of the job I had done on the window screens. He said I did such a great job that I could do all the screens in the house today for him.

Arrrrgggg.

As I worked on the window screens, I smiled the whole time. I didn't need any hassles from Dad. Or Mom.

When I was out back finishing the last ones as it started to get dark, Mom came out. She was on her cell. She walked to the far corner of the backyard and talked on it for a while, giving me the side eye every once in the while. I acted like I didn't notice.

After the call, something weird happened.

Mom walked straight to me and asked me what Stinky's last name was again. I asked her why. She said she always wanted to know the names of the people I was hanging around with. It seemed like a normal enough thing for a mom to do, but since she was typing it into her phone, I knew it was bad.

It didn't take an idiot to figure out that she had mentioned Stinky's name to Stefan. He must have heard the name Van Helsing and had a fit. I'm sure it was a name he didn't like to hear. He must have wanted Mom to find out for sure.

"Sure, Mom," I said, looking her straight in the eye. "His name is Stinky Van . . . Halen."

I never knew that Dad playing all those old rock bands for me all the time would come in handy and maybe save my life, but he loves Van Halen and I had to listen to Eddie Van Halen's guitar solos over and over with Dad.

You never know, do you?

Then she asked how to spell it. She didn't even put it together. This is not good. She typed in her cell and put it into her pocket. Stefan would get the wrong name. For now.

I thought I'd better tell Stinky about it tonight.

March 31.

Time to escape. At about 12:30, after I was sure Mom and Dad were asleep, I snuck out the window. I wore two pairs of pants this time so the rose bushes wouldn't get me again.

After I stashed one pair, I rode my bike to the park to meet Stinky. I went the long way so I wouldn't go by the old State Building and be seen. When I got to the park, Stinky was waiting just where he said he would be.

"They're already out putting up their posters," he said quietly. "We'll have to be careful."

"How many did you see?" I asked.

"First there were four, then there were three. They had their arms filled with blood drive posters. One of them put a poster up right there." He was pointing behind me. I turned to see the poster stapled to the tree in front of me. And a large pile of dust at the base of the tree and the remains of a balloon.

"He didn't even see me," he said proudly. "I watched him walk right over and put up the poster."

"Nailed him in the back, didn't you?" I asked.

"A Van Helsing never attacks from the back. That's cowardly."

"Wow," I said. "You faced him down?"

"Nah. I hid up in the tree and dropped it on his head." He giggled.

I walked over to the pile of dust and kicked it. "Two down."

It was time to get to work. Time to pull those posters down. We split up to work faster. We would meet in an hour to see who tore down the most.

I got on my bike and started down Miller Street. I got a poster from every third telephone pole. I covered six blocks in that hour and got more than forty posters. I got so carried away stealing posters, I didn't notice I was being followed until it was too late.

I got back to the park before Stinky and sat down to wait for him. I heard a noise behind me. "Stinky?" I said. "I got a bunch of them. No way you beat me. How'd you do?"

And out of the bushes walked . . . Rocco.

Rocco?

"Your time is up, Trueheart," he said.

I think I rolled my eyes. "Don't you ever give up?"

He pointed down to his pants. "And I checked my zipper."

"Tell me you haven't been following me all night."

He grinned. "Yep. And after I pound you, I'm calling the cops and telling them you took all those signs down."

I raised my hands in surrender. "Look. If I let you hit me twice, can you not tell anyone what you saw?"

"Do I look stupid to you?" Rocco said.

I wanted to say "Yes," but I remembered from biology that you don't tease wild animals. But he did just stand there looking at me, probably seriously considering my offer.

While he was overworking his brain, there was more rustling in the bushes. Maybe Stinky was there to save me. Or at least to distract Rocco so I could make a run for it.

No such luck. Over Rocco's shoulder I saw a pair of glowing red eyes in those bushes. I think Rocco saw the look on my face as I pointed behind him. "You ain't foolin' me again," he said.

I scanned the ground for a weapon. They were out of reach. I looked back up at my big dumb stalker.

"Rocco," I said, "Listen to me. Get outta here now if you want to live."

"Yeah, right. Like you could do anything to me. I'm ready this time."

"Maybe I can't do anything to you, but he can." I pointed over Rocco's shoulder again. Rocco, unable to resist, turned and looked. He saw the eyes, too. He turned and looked at me, all scared.

"What the hell is that?"

The vampire chose that moment to stride out into the light. He was the biggest guy I had ever seen, kind of like a blood-sucking body builder. He had long blond hair and muscles that bulged out of his T-shirt. I wanted to run, but I couldn't. I knew he'd catch me.

Unbelievably, Rocco chose that moment to get his bully attitude back. "This is a private matter. Buzz off."

He was as dumb as he looked.

The vampire ignored Rocco completely and looked straight at me. "Why did you tear down those posters?"

I stepped toward the vampire. Nothing to lose now. "No blood drive," I said. "No blood. You and your blood guzzling friends will starve."

The vampire smiled. That scared me more.

"Interesting," he said. "Stefan was right. He said somebody was on to us. He'll be glad it was only a kid. He's known since Stanley disappeared."

I started to laugh.

It made him mad. "You think this is funny?"

"Stanley?" I laughed even more. "His name was Stanley? Wow—a vampire named Stanley." I couldn't help myself.

"Vampire?" Rocco said. We both ignored him.

"Go on and joke," the vampire said. He was getting madder. I stopped laughing. "It will be the last joke you ever make."

Rocco stepped up to me. "Who is this?"

The vampire looked at us both. "Someone you don't want to mess with."

And for the first time in this whole deal, I saw fangs. Not little doggie fangs like Half-Whit, but great big vampire fangs. The vampire hissed, opened his mouth and showed them to us. He was going to use them on us, too. I think Rocco screamed. I'm not sure because I know I was screaming in my head. I have never been that scared. Okay, since the alley.

Rocco said in a little tiny voice, "Can I go now?"

"Oh, it's too late for that," the vampire answered. Rocco started shaking.

Then . . . a voice from nowhere. "Hey, Muscle Head! Your friend screamed before he turned to dust. What'll you do?"

It was Stinky. Out there in the dark. The vampire turned to where his voice came from, and I heard the pop and hiss of the air gun. The vampire grabbed his shoulder where he was hit.

He laughed and yelled out into the darkness at Stinky. "Silver bullets only work on werewolves, son."

Oh, no. Tell me no. Werewolves are real, too? More spinning brain time for me. I looked at Rocco. He was still frozen in fear.

Then he kinda turned and looked at me and said, "What's going on?" I may have actually felt sorry for him right then.

Out of the dark, Stinky yelled back at the vampire. "It's not a silver bullet, Dopey."

The vampire thought for a second, then reached to his shoulder and pulled the wooden pellet from it. He looked at it for moment and then he understood. He looked out into the trees.

"Wait! WAIT!" he yelled and started to move his hand to cover his heart.

Too late. The pop and hiss of another shot. The vampire turned and looked at me and Rocco, sheer terror on his face. He moved his hand and I saw a little hole right where his heart should be.

Then he burst into blue flames. Blue. Big blue flames. No heat. Just huge flames up into the trees. And then, he was gone. Just gone. It was awesome. Rocco screamed again. This time I heard it clearly.

Stinky came into the clearing, pellet gun in his waistband, a water balloon in each hand. "That was INCREDIBLE," he said.

I dropped to my knees. "I can't take any more of this."

Rocco woke up. "Take any more of WHAT?"

Stinky grinned. I looked past him and saw two more vampires coming out of the bushes. I jumped up.

"RUN!" I yelled, pointing behind Stinky.

One of the vampires grabbed at Stinky. Stinky ducked him. The other one grabbed Rocco and held him. Rocco struggled and screamed. Stinky threw a balloon at the one holding Rocco and missed, but it hit a tree and splashed on the vampire's back, burning him. He let go of Rocco and spun around a couple of times, smoke coming from his back.

"RUN!" I yelled again at Rocco and Stinky. And we did. All three of us. Both vampires, even the one who was smoking from his back, chased us. Stinky threw his last balloon onto the grass in front of them and they had to stop or get their feet burned off. That gave us enough time to get away.

For a short time.

We all got out of the park and on to a downtown street. As we turned a corner, I looked back and saw both vampires come out of the park. I don't think they saw me.

We ran down the street until Stinky couldn't run anymore. He's got to get into better shape.

As I was catching my breath, Rocco touched my shoulder. "Am I dreaming?" he asked. He looked kinda lost. It was pathetic. At least he seemed like a real person now.

I said, "Nope. You let your lust for revenge on me get you in the middle of this little feud me and Stinky are having with some undead guys."

"Can I leave now? I'll never bother you again." He was sincere.

Stinky piped up. "I don't think so. Those guys will drink your blood before you can get to the corner." Not a smart thing to say.

Rocco started crying. I went up to him. "Cut it out, Rocco. We don't need this right now." I looked at Stinky. "Think of something. He's losing it."

Stinky leaned on a lamp post, thinking. I looked back behind us. The vampires turned the corner and saw us. I turned back to Stinky, pointing at them. "And you'd better think fast."

Stinky looked back at them walking, not even running, toward us. They knew we couldn't escape them.

Stinky looked down the street and saw something he must have liked, because he pumped his fist and went, "YEAH!" and ran off.

Leaving Rocco and me there.

"Hey!" I yelled. I ran off to catch him, pulling Rocco behind me.

Stinky stopped in front of a store. He looked up and smiled. I looked up, too. Rocco didn't do anything. He was useless.

A big sign hung over the business. "Becky's Tanning."

"What?" I asked.

Stinky didn't take time to answer. He picked up a news rack and with it, he busted in the glass front door of the tanning place.

"What are you doing?" I yelled. "We'll get arrested."

"You think arrested is worse than dead? I don't."

Stinky knocked the loose glass out of the door. He looked at me and gestured for me to go first. I wasn't going to argue. I ducked my head and went inside.

Stinky shoved Rocco in and then followed.

We ran upstairs. Well, we pushed Rocco in front of us. There was a hallway. Stinky ran ahead and opened the doors until he found what he wanted and motioned us in. Inside the big room was a single tanning bed. Stinky ran over to it and turned it on.

"What are you doing?" I asked.

We could hear the vampires in the store now, looking for us. Tearing the place apart. Rocco looked at me and said in a tiny voice, "Please save me." Then he lay down on the floor and rolled up in a ball. There was nothing we could do for him.

Stinky looked at me. "Help me push him into a corner. Out of the way."

"Out of the way of what?"

He started pushing Rocco. I helped. Good thing it was a tile floor. Rocco slid pretty easily across the room and into a corner.

"Out of the way of what?" I asked again.

Stinky didn't answer.

He just grabbed me and shoved me toward the tanning bed. He opened it and looked at me. "Get in. Keep your eyes closed. Open it up when I tell you to."

I must have hesitated for a second. He shoved me harder. "I'm not kidding. Get in. It's our only chance."

I've read since that people do crazy things under pressure. I believe it. I lived it. I got in the tanning bed. Stinky closed it on me.

There I was lying in the bed. Getting a tan. I opened my eyes once, but the light was so bright, I closed them again. It was quiet, too.

Then I heard a voice. It was one of the vampires talking to

Stinky. He said, "Sacrificing yourself for your friends? How noble."

Stinky was calm. He said, "My friends are here."

There was quiet for a moment. They're killing Stinky, I thought. I'm next. Or maybe I'm next after Rocco.

But Stinky yelled, "Jess! Come on out!"

I opened the tanning bed and sat up. "You rang?" It was all I could think of.

Both vampires screamed as the UV rays from the tanning bed struck them. Stinky was a genius. He got them into artificial sunlight, and it worked.

Both vampires started to blister and smoke. One of them ran to the door to get out but Stinky headed him off and pushed him toward the tanning bed as I jumped out.

The other vampire headed to the window and broke it trying to get out. He got half way out and exploded.

He blew up . . . and blew out the window and some of the bricks on the outside of the building, too. We heard it all land on the street. It knocked me and Stinky and the other vampire down to the floor. It also woke Rocco up. He started to move again.

Stinky and me got up. "Help me!" Stinky yelled, and we both picked up and shoved the other smoking vampire inside the bed and closed the lid. The tanning bed started shaking and smoke started leaking out the side.

Rocco sat up and looked at us and then at the tanning bed, which was now bucking and smoking big time.

"It's not a dream?" he asked.

"We need to get out of here. Now!" Stinky yelled. I pulled

Rocco up and we all ran down the stairs as fast as we could and out into the street just as the whole top of the building exploded off.

And I mean exploded off. We were ducking pieces of Becky's. Rocco stood there like a statue watching the building parts rain down around him. None of them hit him. It was like he was protected or something. I grabbed him again and pulled him away. I felt kinda responsible for him now.

Afterwards, when I thought about it, I really didn't have to be responsible for him because he had originally come to knock my head off. But then I thought more and figured that wasn't bad enough for me to let him get drained of blood. Sometimes I think too much, I think.

We ran to the other side of the street and stopped for a moment to look at the building because it was really cool to see an explosion like that in real life and not have it crush you, but then we heard sirens and took off.

We stopped around the corner. We saw the lights of the fire trucks and police cars go by and we all looked at each other.

"Did we just blow up Becky's?" I asked Stinky. "Was that real?"

Stinky looked back where we came from. "Technically, the vampires blew up Becky's, not us. But I guess my mom is gonna have to get her tan someplace else for a while."

"Mommy?" Rocco said. His eyes were glassed over. He was completely gone. We had to get him home.

That ended up being pretty easy. If we'd had Half-Whit's

leash, it would have been super easy. I said to Rocco, "Take us to your house." He held his arm out and I took him by the wrist, pushed him ahead of us a little, and we just followed. He never said anything all the way there.

We left him on the porch. I wanted to ring the doorbell, but Stinky said it would be better if we were out of sight when they found him. I agreed. He'd wet his pants, too. I mean, he was a mess. I didn't want to have to explain it. Or make up more lies to cover it.

As we walked back to my house, Stinky smiled at me. "I don't think you're gonna have to worry about Rocco anymore."

"I just hope he's okay. You think he's gonna tell anybody what happened?"

"Let him. Nobody will believe him, plus he won't want to get blamed for Becky's."

"You know, he may not even remember," I said. "He was pretty out of it." Stinky nodded in agreement.

We walked a little more, without talking. Something was bothering me. "Hey," I said, "How come the one guy blew up a little and the other guy took out the building?"

Stinky stopped. "Well, my dad says that the longer they've been vampires the bigger they blow up."

"What? That's stupid."

Well? It is stupid. And I didn't believe him.

"Hey. I don't make the rules." He started walking again.

We finally got to my house. All the lights were still off. They didn't know I was gone, I hoped. I turned to Stinky and said in a low voice. "What now? We just blew up downtown. It's gonna be hard to top that."

He got a serious look on his face. "I don't know what you're doing, but I'm calling the newspaper later and cancelling the blood drive, for starters."

He just doesn't give up. "Be careful" I whispered.

He gave me the thumbs up and walked off.

I was able to sneak back into the house just in time to get ready for school.

Once I got to school, I fell asleep in four of my classes. But I was awake enough to know Rocco didn't come to school.

But worst of all was P.E., where I fell asleep while playing in a basketball game. The P.E. teacher didn't even get mad. She said that in thirty years of coaching it had never happened before. She did ask me to get more sleep at home. I probably played better asleep than I did awake anyways.

April 1.

I dreamed that all the vampires came over and we worked out all our problems. They turned out to be real nice. They offered me a big cup of blood to celebrate.

I was having a great time until Stinky came up to me with his arm around Stefan, showed me his vampire fangs and hissed, "April Fools."

I woke up covered with sweat. I think Half-Whit was sweaty, too.

After a shower, I went down for breakfast. Dad and Lily were already eating.

“Do you want some cereal?” Lily asked, smiling.

“Sure,” I said. So I poured myself a big bowl of cornflakes, loaded on the sugar and milk, took a big bite and screamed. Lily had replaced the sugar with salt.

“APRIL FOOLS,” she yelled. Only Dad kept me from killing her.

Dad also said that someone blew up a building downtown. He heard it on the radio, and everyone was talking about it. He said I should be careful going downtown for a while until they figure out what happened.

He said he bet it was the owner of the building who did it for the insurance. I said, “I bet not.” Then he did what I didn’t want him to. He asked, “Okay. Who do you think it was?”

Oh, man. Not smart on my part. How was I going to get out of this?

Then it occurred to me that this was my opening. My chance to see how far I could go to tell him the truth. “I think it might have been vampire hunters in a life-or-death battle with the undead.”

He looked at me like I was from Mars or something. That didn’t stop me.

“Really. It could have been that. And the vampires exploded.”

Well, that didn’t work. He laughed. He told me if I’d written stuff like that, I might not have flunked creative writing in summer school last year. Then he went back to reading the paper. I reminded him again that I got a D.

But . . . Stinky is right. He’s never going to believe us.

It was a long day at school again, too. I may have fallen asleep a few more times. Everyone was April Fooling each other all over the place. Principal Fellows had to get on the loudspeaker and tell everyone to cut it out. They just laughed.

Danielle said Kenny wanted to draw a mustache on me while I slept in English, but she stopped him.

Neither Stinky nor Rocco were at school. I worried about that. Not Rocco, Stinky. I'd be surprised if Rocco ever came back.

I looked all over the place for Stinky, thinking, this is not good.

On the way home from school I even went by his house. No one was there. Was I on my own now? It was hard not to cry.

At home after school, I knew I couldn't try and call him, or Mom might hear. It was frustrating.

Plus, it was a school night for Mom, so it was double frustrating.

She left. Dad had work to do. So that meant I had to watch Lily. Like the worst torture you can give me. It didn't give me any time to try and call Stinky either.

After I finally got Lily to bed, I ended up waiting for Mom with Dad. He actually asked me to. As it got later, I thought he'd make me go to bed, but he didn't. We talked about a whole bunch of stuff. He asked if I liked any boys from school and junk like that. It was icky, kinda, but I get that he loves me and wants to know more about me.

I told him Kenny wants me to be his girlfriend, but I'm not gonna do that. Dad relaxed for a minute and smiled. "Good for you," he said. We didn't say anything for a few minutes, and then he said, "Can we talk about Abraham? I don't think he's a good influence. I'd really like you to stay away from him."

That just made me think I hadn't heard from Stinky at all today. "I like him, Dad. But not that way because . . . we're friends. Real friends. If you got to know him, you'd like him. I promise. He's not what you think."

"Wow," he said. "I never heard you talk this way about anyone before. I still have my doubts. I want you to think about maybe not hanging out with him. Just my two cents."

If he's lying in a ditch without any blood left in him that won't be a problem, I thought.

What I really said was, "Okay, Dad. I'll think about it." Not even close to the same thing.

We sat and talked some more about school and music and his work. Dad kept looking at his watch the whole time. I knew why.

Mom had been coming home later and later from school. Dad isn't dumb. He saw it. I keep expecting him to tell her to knock it off, but he hasn't. I didn't get it.

When she got home, Dad told me right away to go to bed. I thought maybe he was going to say something to Mom, but he didn't tell her to cut it out, not that I heard. I did get a chance to look at her neck before I left. No new marks. Yay. Double yay. Some good news.

Took me a while, but I finally went to sleep and woke up to knocking on my window. Uh oh, I thought. Vampires? They got Stinky and now they're here for me.

I looked around for a weapon. Zero. The water balloons were in the garage fridge hidden by the outdated juice, and I had no garlic because I was too dumb to remember to get it. So, I picked up my old badminton racquet from the closet and held it up to hit anyone who tried to get in. If they really had gotten Stinky, they'd be in a fight to get me.

More knocking.

I moved the curtain, and it was Stinky, and he was smiling. He looked at me there in my PJs, holding the racquet, and he doubled over, silently laughing. I probably did look ridiculous.

I opened the window. "Don't scare me like that," I whispered.

"Come on," he said. "We've got work to do."

"Why weren't you at school? I was worried sick."

He actually blushed, kinda, in the moonlight, I think. "You were?"

I might have rolled my eyes. Not good.

He saw and snapped out of it. "Dentist."

"Okay. Let me get out of these PJs," I said. Stinky's eyes kinda lit up. We needed to have a talk. I rolled my eyes again and pulled the drapes closed.

That night Stinky and I were out again pulling down posters and again, we split up. I was way more careful this time. I made sure no one was following me. We didn't think any vampires were out anyway.

Stinky even went over to the old State Building and checked it out. There was a vampire standing guard outside. Stinky said they were probably staying inside until they could figure out what was happening to their friends. It must have been driving Stefan crazy. It also meant they would never know we were screwing up the blood drive.

I got home early enough to get an hour of sleep.

April 2.

At school, I asked Stinky if he'd called the newspaper because I'd forgotten to ask the night before.

Hey, I was tired. Okay?

Stinky said he was waiting for me to make the call with him. So, we had a fake deep voice contest. Stinky won. Barely. He would call the newspaper and cancel the blood drive.

After school, instead of going right home, we used the old pay phone in front of the convenience store. It's the only one left in town. I was amazed it worked.

It was hilarious, too. Stinky was great.

"This is Stefan, from the community night school," Stinky said in his best deep voice, through a Kleenex over the speaker part of the phone.

That was my idea. I saw it on TV. And besides helping disguise his voice, that phone was filthy.

"I'm calling to cancel this week's blood drive," Stinky went on. "We checked our stock, and we are in good supply. In fact, we may not need any more for the rest of the year. Would you please announce this in your fine newspaper?" He had to keep waving his hand at me to be quiet, I was laughing so hard.

All we could do was hope it worked.

That night, Mom told Dad she was doing an extra credit assignment and needed to go to the school for a little while. The bad news was Lily had a terrible cold. Well, bad news for Mom.

Yeah, I might have let Lily play outside without a sweater when I was watching her. Still, Mom argued with Dad about whether she should stay home or not.

Dad said he had to go out to a dinner meeting for work, otherwise he said he'd stay. Mom kept saying I could watch Lily. Dad said that was fine under regular circumstances, but not while Lily's running a fever. He also asked Mom why she'd even think about going out when she knew that. Then he asked a question I've NEVER heard him ask, but lately had been hoping he would.

"What's wrong with you?"

She felt her neck where the first bites were. Dad didn't notice. I did. I wanted to say something, but Stinky's words were in my head: "Stop. He won't believe you." And I knew he was right because of our recent-Becky's-blew-up talk.

Mom ended up staying home, but I saw her in the backyard on her cell phone again.

It was making me crazy. I went back to my room and tried to talk to Half-Whit about it, but he fell asleep.

I didn't for a long time.

April 3.

I woke up and went out early to get the paper. It took me a while to find it, but there on page 7 was the announcement of the blood drive cancellation. It even had a big black border around it. Stinky's fake deep voice had worked. Or maybe it was the Kleenex.

Mom reads the paper every day. I was sure she would ask

Stefan about it if she saw it. And if the paper was just missing, Dad would call and have another one delivered, because he has before. I was forced to act.

So, I had to cut the announcement out.

Dad opened the paper at breakfast and turned to the page with the hole in it. He immediately blamed me. “What happened here?”

I was ready.

“Current events for school,” I said, not looking up from my cereal.

“Well, next time let me read it first, okay?” He went back to reading. I got away with it. Now, we had to do something about Stefan seeing it.

I found out at lunch that Stinky took care of it. He went over early in the morning and took all the newspapers from the rack in front of the night school, so the vampires couldn’t get one and read it. All was well for now.

In P.E., the girls played field hockey, which is fun, kinda. Rocco and some of his friends were cutting class and they saw me on the field. Tanya was over by the fence goofing off and heard them talking. She came running back, while they were still there, and told me what they said.

“There she is. There’s Trueheart.” One of Rocco’s friends said to Rocco, pointing at me. “Now’s your chance.”

Tanya said Rocco’s face turned white. Tanya said she could see it. She told me Rocco looked at all the guys there and said, “Listen up. All of you. Anyone who bothers her answers to me.

You got that?

Tanya couldn't believe it.

I did.

"What happened?" Tanya wanted to know.

"We bonded over a shared experience," I answered.

"Huh?" Tanya said.

"That's right." Then I looked over to where they were and caught Rocco's eye and waved. He half waved back. Then he left in a hurry. All his followers ran to catch up.

I think my Rocco problem was officially solved. So, chalk up one point for the vampires. Not enough points to keep me from wanting them gone though.

This was the night the blood drive was supposed to start, too. Hope for it being a big bust was high. Mom was working there the first night, so she'd be able to tell me right away how it went. Again, Dad didn't understand why she had to go, but didn't stop her. I knew he was fed up with all her time at the school. I don't understand him.

I made a list of ways I could tell him about what's going on. After I had a dozen ideas written down, I looked at them and they were all lame. So lame. There had to be a way.

Oh, and I forgot to buy garlic powder again. I told myself to write it on my hand tomorrow to remind me.

I waited up for Mom. It wasn't a long wait. She was home before ten.

And she came home mad. She said nobody showed up for the blood drive and the teachers were very disappointed.

What was left of them, I thought, happily.

"Stefan said it was the worst turnout ever. How can people be so uncaring?" Mom asked me and Dad.

Because they don't want to be Vampire Pepsi, I thought, some more, to myself.

Dad just shook his head. "People are busy at night. They should have the drive on the weekend during the day. These guys need better business sense." Mom felt her neck again before she answered, and it gave me a chill. With zero, and I mean ZERO, emotion she looked at Dad with really cold eyes. He had to notice, too.

"And you need to mind your own business," she told him.

I could see Dad was surprised. Mom didn't care. She marched out of the room and down the hall. Dad looked at me. He was thinking hard. I got up to follow her. He stopped me.

"She's tired. Let her go." I think he was talking to himself as much as to me. So, I did something I don't do much at all. I hugged him. Tight.

He was surprised at that, too, for a second, and then he hugged me back. Tight, too. We didn't say anything else.

Later, in bed, as I was thinking about everything and how well we had wrecked the blood drive, I said to myself, "Poor Stefan, no lunch for you tomorrow, huh? Ha-ha."

I wanted to call Stinky and tell him, but I know it's not safe when Mom is home.

Dad would get me that cell phone if he knew I needed it to protect Mom from monsters.

"You're the only other thing I can talk to about this, other than Stinky," I said to Half-Whit. He looked at me, showed me a couple of his teeth, and then put his nose back in my shoe.

April 4.

I found Stinky at school right away and told him we did it. How we spoiled their blood drive. He said that was great, but we better not get too excited. Sooner or later the vampires were going to figure out somebody had messed with it.

"You can't take the food out of someone's mouth without them fighting back. That's why we need to attack them first, before they come after us," he said.

"How do we get them to come back out?" I asked.

"They're not coming back out again until they can feel safe. And you'd better hope they don't come back out now, because when they do, it will probably be to kill us. No—this time we need to go in after them."

"In?" I hoped I didn't hear him right. "Into the State Building? That's the stupidest thing I've ever heard you say."

"Hey, it's the last place they'd expect an attack. They'll be ready for anything else. And I have a way in."

He pulled out a paper and laid it on the table.

You are invited to a special black tie celebration to honor

NANOOK and SADIE O'BRIEN

on the occasion of their

50TH WEDDING ANNIVERSARY

Saturday, April 12th

8:00 pm 'til who knows when

Old State Ballroom

Main Street, Centerville

"What does this have to do with anything?" I said, throwing the invitation back at him. "I don't know these people."

"Who cares? My Mom does and she's not going. We are. It's our ticket into the State Building."

I did know Nanook. Everybody in town does, but not good enough to go to a fancy party for him.

"Get it through your head—we're going to Nanook's party," he said, smiling. "And we'll stay past closing. The party-crashing vampire killers."

"And you have a plan, right?" I MAY have rolled my eyes.

He looked at me with this crazy grin on his face. "You bet."

April 5.

Saturday. Stinky's mom called my mom and asked if I could come over and stay for dinner. It was Stinky's idea and his mom loved it because he didn't ever have anyone over. Plus, I was a girl.

Dad was there. He looked at me and said, "Can we talk about this?"

I begged him, "Give Abraham a chance, please?"

Mom, who wasn't listening to any of this, told Stinky's mom it was fine with her. She ignored Dad and me, just like we weren't there. Dad didn't get mad or anything—he just shook his head and walked out.

"I have to work at the blood drive again tonight," she said to me. "It hasn't been much of a success, but Stefan wants as many donations as he can get. He's so good for the community."

"He sees you more than I do," said Dad from the other room. "It would be nice if I could spend an evening with you once in a while." He was back in the kitchen now.

"Why don't you work at the blood drive, too?" I asked him.

"Oh, no no no no," Mom interrupted. "They have enough volunteers already. Your dad needs to stay here with Lily."

Dad didn't say anything else. He just went out into the garage. I followed him.

"Dad, why don't you give some blood tonight? Stinky, Lily, and I can come along. Then you and Mom can be together."

"Honey," he said sadly, "your mother has made it very clear that she doesn't want me down there. It's better if I stay away." He gave me a pat on the head and went out to mow the lawn.

As I rode my bike to Stinky's house, I was getting madder and madder. This guy. This stupid guy who lives on blood and power? He wants to break up my parents? I've been doing this to save Mom, but now? This is about keeping my whole family together. And alive, if possible. (Well, if we're together and dead it kinda defeats the purpose.)

When I got to Stinky's, I told him about Mom and Dad. He saw how mad I was and told me I had to control my emotions. That made me madder.

Stinky said it was Stefan's influence at work, and Mom had no control. Deep down I knew that, but it hurt so bad to see my parents torn apart by this evil. I think steam was coming out of my ears.

Stinky said I really needed to calm down. We needed clear heads if we were gonna pull it all off.

Stinky and I spent the rest of the day talking about it. His mom fed us some strange eggplant and fish thing for dinner, and I swear she served weeds for the vegetable.

Mrs. Van Helsing was so strange and funny. She showed me pictures of Stinky as a little kid. Played recordings and old videos of him playing the clarinet.

I looked at him and nodded. "Yeah, you do look like a clarinet kind of guy." He made a fist at me and shook it, but he was smiling.

At dinner, after telling stories about their trip to Death Valley, his mother said, "I'm so excited you're a girl." It made Stinky blush again and this time I got to see it in the light. It was semicute for sure.

But my favorite? Every time Stinky told her to cut something out? She looked at him and waved her hand and said, "Pish tosh." It was funny and cute and Stinky had no defense for it. It's my new favorite phrase.

As I was leaving, Stinky said, "I really liked that you came for dinner."

I waved my hand at him and said, "Pish tosh." It was perfect. He laughed.

When I got home, Mom wasn't there. Dad was reading a book, but I knew he was waiting up for her. It was depressing.

Half-Whit and I went outside for his nightly trip, and I remembered I forgot garlic powder again. That was depressing too.

Mom came home super late. I got out of bed to go see her and tripped over Half-Whit. I hit the floor hard. He didn't even move. By the time I got up, I heard Mom close the door to her bedroom.

I've gotta get rid of this dog, I thought. After this is all over.

April 6.

Dad made me breakfast. In my whole life, Dad had never made Sunday morning breakfast. Never ever.

"Where's Mommy?" Lily asked before I could. I knew Mom came home. I heard her.

"Your mother is in bed," he said. "She was up late."

"Is she okay?" I asked.

Dad looked right at me. "It was strange. She woke up this morning, covered her head and asked me to do something about the sun coming through the window. She said it was hurting her. I guess she has a bad headache."

I got up and ran out of the room.

"Where are you going?" Dad yelled after me.

I ignored him and ran down the hall, threw open the door to my parents' bedroom, ran to the bed, and yanked the covers off Mom.

"Jessica!" Mom screamed, "What are you doing?" She was

covering her head with her hands and arms. I could see the light was hurting her. I took her hair and pushed it out of the way. There it was, a Band-Aid on the other side of her neck. Stefan had bitten her again. One more time and I wouldn't be able to save her.

Dad came running in, grabbed me by the shoulders and yanked me off the bed. "Stop this, right now! Get out of here," he yelled.

I was crying as Dad pushed me out of the room. I've never been angrier and sadder at the same time in my life. Then Lily started crying too, but she always cries if someone else does. It didn't help, though.

"What's going on here?" he said to both of us out in the hallway. "And what got into you?" he said directly to me.

"I don't know," I lied to him. I did know. "I'm worried about Mom." That part was the truth. I wiped the tears from my eyes. "You have to help me take care of her."

"Help you? What does that even mean? She's going to be fine. She's just tired," Dad said. "Now go and calm down." He went back to be with Mom.

How could I calm down when my mom was one bite away from becoming a full-fledged blood-sucking undead vampire servant of that rat-faced Stefan? I went to the kitchen to call Stinky. I had to. I had to tell someone. I did remember about the phone, so I was careful about what I said. I told him I needed to see him.

"Is everything okay?" he asked.

"No," I said. "Mom's not well. She hurt her neck again." I knew he would get the drift.

There was a long pause. "Meet me tomorrow morning," he said.

We hung up without saying anything else.

I spent the day waiting for Mom to come out of her room. She stayed in bed until the evening. When she finally got up, she seemed fine. Once again, I knew better. She was always going to be fine at night now. Not the right kind of fine either.

April 7.

Morning. Mom wasn't up yet, which was unusual, when I left a little early for school. She hadn't made my lunch or told me to have a good day or kissed me or anything.

I met Stinky on the football field.

"Are you sure he got her?" he asked.

"Way, way sure," I answered. "She can't stand the light at all, and she didn't make me lunch. He got her all right. I didn't think he could bite her again so soon. You said he couldn't."

"Sorry. It just means we have to act now."

We decided we needed fancy clothes to wear to Nanook's party, after Stinky explained to me what "black tie" on the invitation meant.

I knew I didn't have that fancy a dress. Last one I had like that now fit Lily. Bows and stuff and junk like that. Not as bad as the one dead Grandma bought me, but almost.

I started to object, but Stinky said we'd need to blend in with the party crowd or the plan wouldn't work. And since we didn't have much money, $65 of my birthday money and zero from Stinky, we decided to meet at the thrift store the next day after school.

"Oh, yeah," Stinky said, pulling a piece of paper out of his pocket. "Since you have all the money, would you pick up this stuff at the store for me? We'll need it."

He handed me the list. He had written it on the back of his Geometry homework. He got an A. I don't get how he does it.

"What do we need all this stuff for?" I asked.

"Trust me, we'll need it all in order for my plan to work," he said and walked away.

It was an interesting list of stuff:

1. Two plastic buckets with handles
2. A box of wooden clothes pins
3. A plastic serving tray
4. Red plastic drink cups
5. Wrapping paper and ribbons
6. A jump rope
7. A staple gun
8. Fishing line (heavy weight)
9. A medium sized Thermos

I wasn't sure what he wanted these things for, but everything else he'd tried had worked, so why not?

After school, I went to the dollar store and got all the stuff on

Stinky's list, but they didn't have any one-dollar garlic powder, even though I finally remembered. I had to get some more.

Later, when I got home from school, there was a van parked in the driveway. A guy from a store came over to sell Mom some new drapes and window shades that keep all the sunlight out.

After Dad got home and saw all the samples, he said he didn't think that we needed any new drapes, but Mom said she would use her own money, so Dad couldn't really say anything about it. Once again, Dad was being shut out by Mom.

He spent the evening in his office. I went in there and he was playing some card game on the computer. I felt so bad for him. He didn't know she had no control over herself anymore.

Mom was in the backyard on her cell after it got dark. Dad didn't see because he was in his office. That was a good thing.

I stashed the stuff Stinky wanted me to buy in my closet, then went out and sat close to Dad while he watched TV.

Mom went into her bedroom and stayed there.

April 8.

We got our report cards at school. I got all Bs and one C in English. Not bad grades for me. I even got a B in P.E.

Which is like a total miracle.

Stinky got straight As. I asked him how he did it when he doesn't study at all. "I do it with smoke and mirrors," he said, waving his hands around like a magician.

"Pish tosh," I said.

After school, we went to the thrift store to buy clothes for the party. The lady who helped us was real nice. She was able to find a nice suit right away that fit Stinky. It was a way cool shiny green job. The pants were too long, but he told her he could fix them himself. I guess he sews, too?

Then we found a great tie for him. It had a picture of a Hawaiian hula girl on it and her grass skirt was the same color as Stinky's suit. It was like a perfect match.

Finding a formal that didn't look like an anniversary cake or was "completely inappropriate for someone my age," as the saleslady said, was harder for me.

Finally, after we found nothing except dresses that looked "like retirement home dresses" on me, as the saleslady said, she went into the back and found this really pretty, kinda short formal dress that was blue and had a cool flippy skirt. I actually liked it. And it didn't look too old for me.

It didn't have any price tag on it and because it was so nice, I knew it had to be too expensive even at the thrift store.

"How much is it?" I asked.

I must have looked appropriately pathetic, because she said, "How much do you have to spend?"

I was down to my last thirty-three dollars after paying for Stinky's clothes. So, I said, "Thirteen dollars." You never leave yourself broke—always have at least twenty dollars on you. My Dad taught me that.

"Well," she said, "you're in luck. It's a ten-dollar dress."

I grabbed it and went to try it on. The girl in the next fitting room zipped it up for me. Even back when this thing started, I would never have asked a stranger to do something like that for me. I know that for sure. Mom not being Mom was forcing me to grow up faster.

When I came out of the dressing room, the saleslady grinned at me and said, “Beautiful.”

I looked in the mirror. Okay, as I said before, I don’t like dresses that much. I know. But I liked this one. A lot. It was like it was made just for me.

“You look amazing,” Stinky said. “Amazing.” He said it twice.

“I hope you have some shoes for it,” said the saleslady. “We have some nice low heels, if you don’t.”

I know how to save money. “My mom and I have the same shoe size. I’ll borrow a pair from her.”

All in all, I had to spend twenty-two dollars and forty cents of my birthday money.

I hid the dress in my closet. I knew Mom wouldn’t look there, but I still didn’t want to have to explain it, just in case.

Mom went to class again. Dad was going to let me wait up with him, but Mom came back early. I was surprised. I think Dad was, too.

“What happened to your class?” Dad asked her.

“Stefan had to leave early. He was very upset.”

“What happened?” I asked. I was almost afraid to ask.

“He found out that someone tore all his blood drive posters down and called the newspaper and told them it was canceled. That’s why it was a failure.” She sounded angry.

Uh-oh, I thought.

She looked angry, too.

"Do they know who did it?" I tried to sound cool.

"Probably some practical joker," Dad said. Mom glared at him like she thought he did it.

"No one knows yet, but Stefan says if he finds out, they're in big trouble." She was looking straight at me. I started to sweat. She walked over and put her arm around my shoulder. I started to sweat more.

"Jessica," she said, "Stefan would like you to ask around school and see what you can find out about this."

Yeah, right. To quote Mom herself, "When pigs get wings."

But what I actually said? "Okay Mom, I'll find out what I can." Then I smiled and yawned. "I'd better get to bed now. 'Night Mom, 'night Dad." I casually walked to my room, but I was sweating like I was running.

One good thing? It looked like they didn't know it was Stinky and me. Yet.

April 9.

I didn't see Stinky at school. He got to go on a special field trip to the ballet for getting straight As. I was glad I got that C.

I couldn't see him after school either because Lily and I had to go to the dentist to get our teeth cleaned. Dad took us, too. Lily asked where Mom was, so I didn't have to do it. Dad just told her he wanted to do it. I knew that wasn't true.

I watched Dad while Lily was in there. He looked so sad. I went and sat next to him. We didn't say anything, and I think he was happy about that.

Also, I hate going to the dentist. I wonder if holy water works on them, too.

After the dentist, I went home and got some cereal out to eat. After a good teeth cleaning, I needed some sugar. I went to the cupboard to get some and what do you think I found? A new jar of garlic powder. Right in the front. Mom must have bought it. Maybe she wasn't as affected as I thought. Or maybe it was a trick to see if I'd take it. Is Mom that sneaky? Just in case, I decided to buy my own, just to be careful.

If I could remember.

April 10.

At school, I finally caught up with Stinky. He wasn't worried about the blood drive thing or Stefan knowing we messed with it. Well, he liked them not knowing it was us. He didn't care they knew it happened.

Stinky was really confident. "Nah, he doesn't know it was us or he'd be after us already. We need to concentrate on Saturday."

He told me he needed the stuff on his list to get it ready for the party. "What are you going to do with it?" I asked.

"What do you think? Wipe them out."

When we got back to my house after school, there were a bunch of trucks out front and workmen going in and out. "What's going on?" I asked Mom.

"All the new drapes and window shades are being installed," she told us.

I looked at Stinky and rolled my eyes. I looked back at Mom. That's when I noticed how terrible she looked. Her make-up was all messed up and her hair was combed all wrong.

"You two go to Jessica's room and get out of the way," Mom said to us.

Wait. What? Mom and me had this serious talk the first time I shaved my legs: "No boys in your bedroom."

Now she was sending me there with a boy and looking like she did her hair and make-up in a blender.

"Wow, did you see my mom?" I asked Stinky when we got to my room. I wasn't about to tell him anything about the whole boy/girl bedroom thing. We didn't need that complication.

"Don't you get it?" Stinky said. "She can't see herself well in the mirror anymore. It's all part of the change." I'd forgotten that vampires can't see their reflections. There were so many rules.

"My dad has got to notice all these things sooner or later. He's not blind."

Stinky sat on my bed. "He's already probably noticed, but even then, he'll look for an explanation that makes sense. He'll never believe it's vampires. But if we don't do something, Stefan will finish turning your Mom, and your dad will never see them coming. That's why we have to act."

"And that's fair? To just leave him out? We've got to figure out a way to tell him. I'm not kidding. He's really smart."

"Yes—but we need to leave him out of this. Telling him will just get her killed. Then him. Faster." He was getting mad now.

"I'm not sacrificing my dad, too. You get me?" I was in his

face. He backed away, holding his hands up.

"Hey. I'm not the enemy."

I sat down on the bed next to him. "Yeah. I know . . ."

He got serious. "I wish my dad was here. Maybe your dad would listen to him. All I know is right now, we have to do this alone."

We sat there for a while not saying anything. Then I got up. "I got your stuff in the closet," I said, changing the subject.

"Great. Can you get it for me? I need to go get it ready."

"I wish I knew what you're up to with this stuff." I said, throwing the two shopping bags on the bed.

Stinky looked in the bags. "Don't worry about anything. I have it all under control."

Under control. I was leaving the fate of my family in the hands of a kid who smelled like garlic. A kid who needed fishing line and a Thermos to wipe out vampires. I didn't care what Stinky said. I had to tell my dad. Somehow.

Stinky looked up at my window. The new curtains were already installed. He looked at me and smiled, and then turned and shut them. We couldn't even see each other it was so dark in the room. We couldn't see anything. All I could hear was Half-Whit breathing. That made it scarier. "The sun won't get to her in here," Stinky said, there in the dark. It was creepy.

Mom didn't even see when Stinky left with the shopping bags.

It took the workmen until after Dad got home to finish up. When Mom closed all the new drapes and shades it was so dark you couldn't see your hand in front of your face anywhere in the house. Now the sunlight couldn't get in anywhere to hurt her.

April 11.

It was easy to figure out a way to get out of the house to go to Nanook and Sadie's party. There was a dance at school Saturday night. I'd just tell Mom and Dad I was going to the dance. Even though I'd never gone to one before, and had told them many times I'd never ever go to one in my life, I was sure my parents wouldn't suspect a thing. Yeah, right. Still, it was the best bet to a free pass to get out Saturday.

Mom couldn't have cared less. "Oh. Okay," was all she said.

Dad was a different story. "Okay, what's going on? Where are you really going?" Dad asked when I told him about the dance. He knew me too well.

"I'm going to get all dressed up and go to the dance," I said sincerely.

"And dance?" He had me there. I dance like a floppy fish, mostly, and he knows it. Plus, he had the memory of my telling him never ever.

"Mostly just hang out," I answered.

"I wish I could believe you," he said. "But you've been doing some strange things lately. You? A dance?"

"Dad, please trust me. I need to go to this dance tomorrow night. It's life or death."

"A life-or-death dance? Never heard of one of those before." He put his hand on my shoulder. "Look Jess, I need to know if you're in some kind of trouble. If you are, I'm here to help."

"Okay. Okay. I'm helping a friend. But I promise it's not drugs, it's not gangs, it's not drinking. It's just a friend with some problems." That wasn't a lie. Mom is a friend.

"Is it something you want to talk to me about? Is it Abraham?" he asked. "You know what I think about him."

"No. Pish tosh." It came out of my mouth before I thought about it. Dad laughed. At the "pish tosh," I think. I ignored him and kept talking. "He's just a friend. This has nothing to do with him." Now, that was a lie.

Then he got all serious. "You're not doing anything stupid or dangerous, are you? That's where I'm drawing a line. You're too precious to me."

"Cross my heart," I said. That's not yes or no. So, I didn't really lie. Plus, I like that I'm precious to him. He never said that to me before. Him and Mom are precious to me.

"Okay. Have fun at the dance." He patted me on the head. I hugged him. "I'm here if you need me," he said.

That night in my room, I wrote Dad a letter on one of those yellow legal pads. I told him everything. It took me hours to write. I didn't leave anything out of it. I put in every detail. Red eyes in trees. Melting vampires in the alley. Blowing up Becky's. Rocco wetting himself. Why Mom was acting like a jerk and looked like a bag lady. Everything. He'd need to know all about the vampires if I didn't make it home from the Nanook party. I begged him to please believe it. If I couldn't save Mom, he needed to believe me and do something to save her.

I snuck into his office and put the letter in his briefcase. It would be safe there. Mom never looked in Dad's briefcase.

I felt like I'd just done something wonderful.

And then I did something stupid, radically stupid, bonehead stupid a few hours later.

Why? I thought I had a good reason.

I was late for school, and I ran like crazy to get to math class. When I ran in the room, everybody was already there and Mrs. Ogden, the teacher, was at the whiteboard writing a bunch of letters. Not numbers. Letters.

A

A+

B

AB-

O

O+

And everyone in the class was writing on their papers like their lives depended on it. They didn't even look up at me. I ran to my desk and sat down, hoping the teacher didn't see me.

I watched everybody writing and thought, "Oh, man. Was there a test today?"

I raised my hand and cleared my throat to get Mrs. Ogden's attention. She turned and looked at me. "Yes, Jessica?"

"Could I get a copy of the test please?"

Everybody looked up and laughed. She didn't.

"You didn't do your homework did you?" she said, pointing to the white board.

I didn't understand. "I'm sorry. I didn't have this homework.

What math is this? I studied for the lesson on rational numbers. Is this algebra?" I asked.

She gave me a dirty look, "I'm disappointed in you, Jessica."

"I thought I did the right homework. Honest. I didn't see this at all. What are we supposed to do with these letters?"

Everyone in class laughed, again.

Mrs. Ogden walked down the aisle to my seat in the back. Yes, I always sit in the back. She stood over me.

"This is one third of your grade, young lady, and you didn't do the assignment? Do you not want to pass?"

"Yes, I do. Tell me the assignment. I'll do it at lunch. I promise."

More laughter. Huge laughter.

I stood up and faced her. "What's so funny?"

She was doubled over laughing, and then she stood back up to face me. "The assignment IS lunch. Which blood type tastes the best. Where have you been?"

She smiled. And her fangs showed for the first time. I looked at the rest of the class. They all had fangs, too.

I screamed and pushed Mrs. Ogden away from me and ran out of the room.

At that second, I sat upright in my bed, a sweaty mess. Half-Whit was on the bed with me, sleeping. He didn't even wake up. I was breathing hard. It seemed so real. I was just starting to calm down when someone knocked at my bedroom door. I looked at the clock next my bed and it said 7:11 am. I'd overslept. I sprung out of bed, right over the dog. He didn't even move. "I'm sorry,"

I shouted.

I opened the door and Lily was standing there. Dressed in all black. "Lily? What are you doing?"

"I need my breakfast, Ick-a," she said.

"Then go bother Mom or Dad." I was getting mad.

"No," she said, "You."

"I don't have your breakfast. Okay?" I was shouting now.

"Oh yes, you do," she answered, calmly. And then she opened her mouth and showed me her fangs. They were huge. They were dripping blood. I slammed the door in her face and locked it.

She started pounding on the door. I ran back to the bed and jumped onto it. Half-Whit woke up this time. More door pounding.

"We have to get out of here," I said to him.

He farted and opened his mouth. Fangs. Huge vampire fangs. I screamed louder than I ever have in my life.

I woke up again. This time for real. I pinched myself like twice to make sure. I was so sweaty this time that I needed a towel.

I got up and immediately tripped over Half-Whit, who was on the floor, nose in my shoe. He didn't even wake up, again. It must have been the deep sleep of stupidity.

Well anyways, back to my stupidity. The dream scared me so much I went to the kitchen and called Stinky to make sure he was okay. He answered the phone.

"Stinky," I whispered. "I'm scared. Are we doing the right thing?"

"Go back to bed," he said. "Everything's all right. Those

bloodsucking creeps won't know what hit them."

"I want this to be over. I'm having vampire nightmares."

That's when I thought I heard the click. I hope Mom hadn't heard everything. "Well, goodnight," I said. "See you at the school dance." I said that in case Mom was still listening.

He wasn't done and I couldn't tell him to shut up. "We'll win, okay? It'll be all right. We will destroy them. Now get some sleep. You'll need all your energy. G'night."

When I hung up the phone, my hands were shaking. If she had heard it all, we were toast.

As I walked down the hall back to my room, I noticed Mom and Dad's door was open a crack. Did I see glowing red eyes? I hoped it was just my imagination.

I didn't sleep well the rest of the night. In fact, I got back up and locked my door. Something my parents told me I couldn't do overnight in case of an emergency. Now I was locking it because of one.

April 12.

I was so nervous in the morning that I actually took Half-Whit for a walk. I even let Lily come with me. It didn't help. Lily talked non-stop the whole time and I had to drag Half-Whit most of the way. Plus, I checked Lily's teeth for fangs.

Hey, that dream was too real.

Mom acted okay all day. If she'd heard us, she wasn't letting on at all. She even asked me if I had laundry for her to do. Pretty normal. For a two-thirds vampire.

As I was getting my dirty clothes out of the hamper in my closet for her to wash, I looked at the bag the blue dress was hanging in. Tonight was the night. Do or die.

Then it occurred to me I still didn't have any shoes to wear with the dress. If I wanted to blend in, I couldn't wear what I have. Tennies, sandals, and some ugly flats. It would just look weird with that fancy dress. Stinky said we bought those outfits so we'd blend in. We needed to blend in for important reasons, too. I didn't need to get us killed because I wore the wrong shoes.

I took my dirty clothes to Mom in a big pile. She took them without saying a word. I high-tailed it back to my room and listened at the door.

I had to get into Mom's closet to find some shoes. It would have to be a quick snatch and grab. When I heard the washer start and knew Mom was putting my clothes in, I made a mad dash down the hall into her bedroom.

I went straight to her walk-in closet and right to the shoes. She has a LOT of shoes. Dad says she's a shoe hoarder. Mom says if you buy good shoes (and by "good" I knew she meant "expensive"), and if they look good and feel good, you feel better about yourself. I never really understood that, but she said I'd figure it out as I got older. One more thing I'd know when the time was right. This one was in the shoe category, I guess.

Right now, I needed to grab a pair that would go with the dress. Blue. A pair caught my eye. The blue looked right. Then I heard Dad in the hall. He was talking to Lily because you can't mistake that motor mouth. They passed right by the room on their way to hers to get dirty clothes for Mom.

This was my chance. I grabbed the blue ones, stuck them under my shirt, opened the door to the hall a crack, saw no one, and dashed back to my room.

I hadn't had my door shut a few seconds when I heard Dad and Lily walking back to the laundry room. Whew.

I pulled the shoes out and well . . . they were the cool ones with the wood high heels I used to use to knock over Legos.

I went to the closet and lifted the bag off the dress, and it matched the shoes pretty well. I went and locked my door and tried them on. They felt really good. Then I stood up on them.

Wow. Like walking on stilts. I was really wobbly. Now, like most girls, I had tried on high heels when I was little, but not for years, and because I needed these to work, I spent the rest of the afternoon practice-walking in them in my room.

Half-Whit sat on the bed and watched like I was nuts.

And after a while they did start to hurt a little, but it was okay. I knew I wasn't gonna run in them, because if I was in situation where I had to run, off they were going to go.

Finally, feeling almost comfortable in them, I took them off and looked at them. They were pretty. And you could see the pretty wood grain in the thin heels, classy. One of them still had a little tiny price tag on the bottom. I gasped.

Three hundred and seventy-five dollars? No way! Wow. No wonder she got mad when I knocked over the Lego buildings with them. I never saw her wear them, but I'm sure she did. I hoped so. That's a lot of money.

"They better be comfortable for that price," I thought.

I set the alarm and then lay down to take a little nap. Half-Whit snuggled into me. I didn't mind too much. He only farted bad once.

Beep. Beep. Beep. The alarm went off, waking me up. It was time to get ready for the party. I sat down at my desk and looked in the mirror. Ponytail wasn't going to do it. Grrr.

I brushed my hair. No way did I have the time to curl it, nor did I want to. It kinda has a natural wave, so I was okay. It looked maybe party ready.

My Aunt Shirley gave me some make-up on my last birthday. I hadn't touched it since. I knew it was in my desk because Mom said I couldn't throw it away. I wasn't going to put anything on my eyes, because I knew I'd end up looking like a raccoon. I grabbed the lipstick. It wasn't too red, kinda pink Ewww, pink. Ahhh . . . the things I will do to blend in and save my mom.

I put the dress on. It took me more than a couple of gymnastic moves to get the zipper in the back all the way up. Half-Whit looked like he enjoyed the show.

Finished, I looked in the mirror. One more hair brushing. It kinda looked like me, only girly and pretty. Under heavy interrogation I would have to admit I liked it, a little. I sat down and slipped on the shoes.

I was ready.

As soon as it started to get dark, Mom took off in her car. Out the window from my room I saw her leave. I went out to the living room. Dad was looking out the big window.

"Where's Mom going?" I asked.

"I don't know. The store I guess," he said. "She didn't tell me." That's when he turned around and got a good look at me. His eyes got wide. "Honey? What? Where?" You could see his shock.

"I bought it myself. I didn't have anything to wear to the dance."

"Well, good for you." He laughed. "You look . . . grown up? I'm not sure I'm ready for this."

"I'm not sure I'm ready for this either," I said back. He laughed again.

I excused myself and said I had to go to my room for a second. As I passed the kitchen, I went in and took the jar of garlic powder Mom had bought because I'd forgotten to buy my own— again. It was then I realized I didn't have any pockets. You get used to pockets, and then when you don't have them it's a pain. Oh geez, I was going to have to take a purse.

One more silent trip to Mom's closet and I was holding a little purse, what Mom told me once was a clutch. It was black. Black purse and blue dress. That worked for me because I figured if I was going to fight vampires in this outfit, I might end up black and blue by the end. I put the garlic powder in the purse. That was all I had in there. All I needed.

When I got back to the family room I said, "Dad, I'd better let Half-Whit out to do his thing before I go."

He offered to do it so I didn't mess myself up, but I told him it was my responsibility. Parents always like when you say that and will let you do almost anything when you say it. He let me go.

I picked up my dog and went outside.

Once I was out there, I dropped Half-Whit in the middle of the lawn and quickly put garlic on all the windows and doors. The garlic powder didn't smell exactly the same as before, but maybe it was a different brand. Half-Whit actually got up and took advantage of the opportunity to relieve himself.

We were heading back to the house when Mom drove up. I put Half-Whit down at my feet and waited at the door for her.

"Don't you look nice," she said. Her eyes glowed a little red in the dark. "You are going to the school dance, aren't you? With that nice Abraham?"

"Yep, the school dance. Both of us. I can't wait." I could tell she knew everything. And if she did, so did Stefan.

"Are you going anywhere else? I mean, afterward?" she asked. Stefan must have wanted to know.

"Some of the kids talked about doing something after the dance," I lied. I figured it was all right to lie in this case. I wasn't guilty about this one. If I told her where I was gonna really be, I was dead for sure.

"Something? Like what? Where would you go?" She wanted details. Stefan was going to come after me tonight. I knew it. I had to throw her off.

"The arcade, miniature golf, ice cream, I don't really know. I'll call you when I do. I wouldn't go anywhere without telling you, you know that." Except maybe to fight vampires.

"Good, you do that. You call." She walked into the house and left me alone on the porch.

She KNOWS I don't have a cell phone and can't call her.

Scary.

"She's almost gone, isn't she?" I said to Half-Whit. Half-Whit looked up at me and groaned.

It was time to go.

Dad dropped me off at school around 7:30. There were lots of kids getting dropped off for the dance. "You have fun." Dad said.

"I love you, Dad." I said back. I reached over and hugged him. He hugged me back, then looked at me.

"You sure you're okay?" he asked.

"Go home and look in your briefcase," is what I wanted to say, but instead I said, "I'm fine." I got out of the car, and he took off. He did stop and look back at me once. I waved. He took off. I kicked off the borrowed heels.

I met Stinky on the football field, barefoot, shoes in hand. He had the buckets, his backpack, the Thermos, and two gift-wrapped presents.

"You got any money on you?" he asked.

Money. I remembered garlic powder in my purse, but not money. "Don't you have any money?" I asked.

He ignored me. "Good. I ordered a cab. Grab a bucket. He's meeting us at the corner."

I picked up the bucket. It was heavy, but it didn't feel like liquid. "What's in this?" I asked him.

"I froze the holy water to make it easier to transport. It'll melt by the time we need it." Stinky's mind works overtime, I think.

He held up the gifts. "These packages will get our stuff into the building easier. People will just think they're presents for the

O'Brien's. We're covered."

I had my purse, my shoes, and a bucket of frozen holy water. And a fancy dress. What could go wrong?

We told the driver to take us to the Grand Theatre. It's a block away from the old State Building.

After the driver dropped us off, Stinky paid, but he wasn't happy. I think he thinks I'm the money and he's the brains.

We walked down one block and then over one block so that we could come in from the back of the State Building. You could see it was pretty well lit in front, but from the back we could sneak down the side of the building in the dark easily, and then slip in the front.

I had to be careful I didn't get my dress messed up or my feet too dirty. He didn't care about his clothes. Being a real girl is more work than being a guy.

As we got closer to the front, we left the buckets, the backpack, and the Thermos in the bushes near one of the lower windows. Stinky said we could pass them through the window later.

Then we took a present each and headed toward the front door. Stinky was walking ahead of me. Suddenly, he threw himself down, flat on the ground.

Now, I'd gotten to know Stinky well enough to understand that when he did something like this, I should pay attention. I went down on my stomach, too.

Well, not really. The dress. So I was on my toes and elbows. We were on the ground in the shadows of the concrete stairs that led up to the front of the building.

Stinky used his hand nearest me to point up. I looked up, trying not to move my head too much. Above us, standing at the top of the stairs was Stefan and another guy.

Stefan was talking. "Sandra says they'll be at their school dance tonight. She gave me a map of the school."

"Excellent," said the other creep.

"Sandra? That's my mom," I whispered to Stinky. I looked back up at them.

"I'm going over there to wait for them to come out," said Stefan. "I want to take care of this myself. Do you want to join me, Leopold?"

"Is that an invitation to dinner?" Leopold chuckled and a chill went up my spine. They were talking about my blood.

"It's going to be a pleasure to kill a Van Helsing," Stefan hissed.

"What if they're not there?" Leopold asked.

"Sandra said they'd be at one of those places kids hang out these days. I have a list. We'll look until we find them. We have all night." Stefan stretched his arms out, opened his mouth and hissed again. Then he said, "Let's go put a stop to those annoying brats."

They both started laughing and walked down the steps, out into the night.

Stinky and I stayed there on the ground for another fifteen minutes at least, just to make sure they were gone. Stinky finally spoke, doing his best Stefan imitation. "It's going to be a pleasure to kill a Van Helsing." He sat up. He was mad. "Boy, I'll tell you,

Jess—I'm going to melt that guy like a grilled cheese sandwich. Nobody threatens my family like that."

"Mine either," I said.

"Speaking of your family, your mom ratted us out."

I got up. "Yeah. Sorry about that. She can't help it, though. But it tells me she's capable of anything if she'd just let them kill me. I'm more worried than ever now, about Dad and Lily. Aren't you worried about your mom?"

He nodded. "Yeah. That's why we have to finish this tonight."

"But they know about us."

"Don't worry. It doesn't change a thing. They know about us now, but they don't know we know they know."

I started slipping on my shoes. "What?"

He rolled his eyes. "Come on. We have a party to go to." He stood up, dusted himself off, walked up the stairs, and went into the ballroom. Without me.

Some date.

I grabbed the presents, my purse, wobbled on the heels for a second, got my balance, shook my hair out, and then walked up the stairs pretty well. I stood looking at the doors for a second. Is this my last night on earth? I wondered. If it was, I vowed to take as many of those vampires with me as I could.

I focused on my reflection in the glass door. I still looked pretty darn good for what I'd been through so far. Now, I said it out loud. "This is for you, Mom." I opened the doors.

It was very crowded inside and the party was going full blast. A band was playing on one side of the room. A really bad band with, like, forty saxophones. It sounded like music my grandmother would have loved if she wasn't dead. A bunch of people were already dancing, ignoring how bad it was. Stinky was nowhere to be found. I looked out into the crowd, trying to spot him.

"There's a table to put your gifts on," said a lady when I held them out to her. She motioned to the table.

"Thank you," said a voice behind me. Stinky was back.

I put the packages on the table. "Where did you go? Don't leave me alone like that." I stared at him.

"I found a broom closet in back. We can stash the presents in there until we need them. In fact," he said, looking around the room, "it's so crowded in here, I think we can go out and bring the rest of the stuff through the front and no one will notice."

He was right. We didn't even have to use the window. Stinky went out and brought the buckets and the backpack right in through the front door. Everybody was so busy having fun that no one noticed him bringing the stuff in or us putting it all in the broom closet.

Then Stinky made me go steal my gift back from the table. He said if a pretty girl did it and got caught, they'd believe any story she made up.

He was right. I told this lady who saw me taking it that my parents wanted to give it to Nanook and Sadie themselves because it was too valuable to leave on a table.

"Pretty smart of them," she said. "I may have to get mine off there, too. You never know what kind of people come to something like this in a public place."

I smiled and batted my eyes at her. I have no idea why, it just seemed right. It worked. And I kinda felt icky about it. The woman walked off to get her present, I think, and left me there to go back to our closet.

"You were right again," I said to him as I handed him the present. His mind was elsewhere.

"Let's have some food. It looks great," Stinky said.

He was right. Again. The food was indeed awesome. Nanook and Sadie O'Brien owned the best Chinese restaurant in town. And even though he was half-Eskimo and half-Irish, he made the best Mu Shu Pork I have ever tasted. Our family ate there at least once a month and always had a great time. Thinking about it made me sad. Mom was Mom then. Thinking about the Chinese food made me miss her and want her back.

Not enough not to eat it.

Anyways, the remaining vampires were easy to spot. They all had on gray coats with white aprons. They were serving at the Chinese buffet or serving drinks at the bar. One of them was serving drinks from a tray. I think he was the only one doing that.

"Watch what that one does for a while," Stinky said pointing to the one with the tray. Then Stinky disappeared into the crowd. So, I watched the guy. It was boring. I knew he was a vampire, probably, but that didn't make him any less boring.

The guy would go to the bar, get a tray full of drinks, pass them out quickly, take back some empty glasses, and go through a door I assumed was the kitchen. Then he'd come back out with an empty tray and get more drinks from the bar. I watched him do it a bunch of times.

I was watching him do it for the eleventh time (yes, I was actually counting), when Stinky came back with his own tray of glasses, with the red plastic cups I'd bought, filled with water. "Here, take this." He handed me the tray.

"What for?" I asked. "Do I look like a waiter?"

He looked me over. "No, you look like a princess," he said, smiling. "But tonight, you'll be serving the house special—holy water cocktails."

Ah ha. He used the glasses, the tray, and the Thermos for this. Three of the items on his list. Three items I'd bought. That now I was going to use.

I waited until the vampire waiter guy went into the kitchen again and then I followed him in with my own special tray.

"You want these in here?" I asked him. I must have startled him because his feet slipped a little as he turned to face me.

"There's no need for you to do this," he said seriously. "You shouldn't even be back here."

"No kidding," I said. "These slippery floors could be dangerous." I started walking toward him, wobbling a little in the heels. This worked to my advantage.

"Please put those down. I'll take care of them." He backed up a little.

I kept walking toward him. He kept backing up. Finally, his back to a wall, I yelled, "WHOOPS," and spilled the whole tray of drinks all over him. I got him good. He dropped his tray and looked at me for a millisecond, spun around a couple of times and then he—and his clothes—collapsed into a pile of dust. I was afraid the smoke detectors would go off. They didn't.

I got a little dust on my dress skirt. I shook it off. Cool. My dress was also vampire dust proof.

I thought I'd better get out of there. As I headed for the door, Stinky came in carrying a broom and dustpan. "You've really gotten sloppy," he said, laughing. "We can't go around leaving a mess now, can we?"

"Listen, I did the hard part. All you have to do is clean it up." I smiled at him and left the kitchen.

He came out a few minutes later carrying the vampire's remains in a trash bag, which he deposited in the nearest can.

"You're supposed to recycle your trash, not throw it away," I said, wagging my finger at him.

"He wouldn't even make good fertilizer," Stinky answered.

"Let's split up and see if they miss him," I suggested. I was getting into this.

I went over by the band. Still bad. Now they had a guy with an accordion playing along with all the out-of-tune saxophones. "They don't play music like this anymore," I heard someone say.

Thank goodness, I thought.

It didn't take long for the remaining five vampires to meet in a corner. I looked around for Stinky so I could tell him. That's when I noticed he was dancing with an older lady right in front of where the vampires were standing. He was pretty good.

After I watched the vampires meet, talk, and split up, Stinky danced his way over to me. "Great music, huh?" he said. We would need to have a serious talk after all this was over. If we were still alive.

"Could you hear what they were saying?" I asked when the song finished and he stopped dancing.

"Not very well, but they seemed upset." He wiped the sweat from his forehead. "Boy, that lady can dance."

Stinky leaned in and said it was time to set another trap. He went to the broom closet and came back with one of the buckets. The ice had completely melted. I do think Stinky is some kind of genius.

"See that third door over there?" he said, pointing to a door at the back of the room. "Wait about five minutes, then go get the guy at the buffet table. All you have to do is get him through that door, any way you can, and into the hall. I'll do the rest." He already knew where the doors went. He'd studied the floor plan his dad had. Why he gets As and I get Cs. I'm glad he does.

So, I waited the five minutes. It seemed like an hour. But I figured it would give me time to think of something foolproof to say. But no.

As I waited, leaning against the wall, watching the clock and thinking, this kid walked up to me. Okay, he wasn't a kid; he must have been sixteen or seventeen or something. He was wearing like, a full-on tuxedo and looked—okay, really good.

"Hi," he said.

"Hey," I answered. A really clever comeback, huh?

"Uhhh, I saw you—well, my mom saw you across the room, and you know, I agreed you looked all alone and we—that is, I—thought you'd like to talk or maybe dance." He wasn't as smooth as he looked. Plus, his mom?

He was cute though. And . . . under regular circumstances where I wasn't going to leave him in a few minutes to go kill an undead monster, I might want to get to know him. Maybe. But it wasn't regular circumstances.

I gave him my best *I wish I could* look and said, "I can't right now. I'm meeting someone in a couple of minutes." It was true, but it sounded like a lie. I can't win.

Here's where I tell something else that's true. This was the very first time an older boy ever wanted to talk to me other than to make fun of my middle name. So, it wasn't a horrible thing. It was actually that first moment as a semi-adult person you wait for, kinda, when you daydream sometimes, but never tell anyone else about it. And now it was happening, and I had to vaporize vampires that were trying to kill me instead of dancing like a floppy fish with this guy.

"I'm Jessica," I said. Holy crap. Really? I said that? And, "Maybe . . . next time?"

"Okay, Jessica. That's a deal. I'm Brad," he said. But I could see he was disappointed. He even looked back at his mom and shrugged. Brad. I love that name, too. Oh, well. Wasn't really a choice. It was kill or be killed, so Brad had to go. Doesn't mean I wouldn't look for him in town again. But then, I'd look fourteen again, too. Grrrr.

He turned and walked back to his mom. I looked back at the clock. It was time.

So, I messed my hair up a little and ran over to the buffet table. “Mister, mister, some guy cut himself real bad back there. There’s blood everywhere.” I pointed to the door. His eyes lit up. I had him.

“Where?”

“Follow me!” I ran toward the door and went through. There was a short hall leading to another door.

“Where?” he said again, coming up behind me.

I pointed to the door. “In there—but I can’t go in. There’s too much blood. I might get sick.” I was holding my hand over my mouth.

“Yes,” he said. “You stay out. I can take care of the blood.” He rushed through the door.

Stinky had balanced the bucket on top of the door, so when the vampire went in, the water and the bucket came splashing down. Instantly, he was smoking and screaming, the blue bucket covering his head. Soon, the bucket was sitting on a big pile of dust.

“They’re not paying me for this extra housekeeping duty,” Stinky said, broom in hand.

“They’re not paying you at all,” I said.

We cleaned up the mess quickly, deposited the vampire in the trash, and got back to the party. Nanook was making a speech. Everyone was clapping and having a good time. Nobody had heard the vampire screaming. Of course, the bucket on his head had muffled the sound pretty good.

We watched as the four remaining vampires got together and stayed together. They had to figure something was wrong. They even left the ballroom and were gone for quite a while. We thought they were probably searching for the other two.

"They should check out the trash cans," I said.

It was getting late when they came back into the ballroom. The party was breaking up. Nanook and Sadie had opened their presents, the band had played its last song, and people were leaving in groups.

I was standing close to Stinky when Brad and his family walked by, leaving. Brad looked at Stinky in his green suit and hula tie and I think he reassessed his thoughts about me. Stinky watched this and looked at me. "You know that guy?"

I shook my head. "Nope. Probably never will now."

Stinky said, "Huh?"

I looked at him. So earnest, risking his own life to help me save my family and I thought, Brad's got nothing on you. I grabbed his hand. "What next?" I asked.

"We need to hide out for a while, until they close the place up," Stinky said, holding my hand harder.

"No," I said. "Listen to me. I've been thinking about this. We got a couple of them by surprise. There are too many of them, if we're here alone."

He dropped my hand. Dropped it. "You don't get it, do you?" he said. "This is the last stand. We have to see this through, or we're done. Stefan knows who we are. You heard him."

I looked at him in his shiny green suit and down at me in my blue dress. "Okay. You're right, but it's going to be kind of hard to hide out in here when we look like a couple of popsicles."

"Good point. I'll lose my coat," he said. He took it off.

"I can't take anything off," I said.

He looked at me and smiled. "Remember, you're a pretty girl. If we get caught you can get away with most anything as far as I'm concerned."

Because I'd never really been a pretty girl before, the idea of using something like that to get away with stuff? Ewww. Mom taught me better than that. But then I used it on the lady at the gift table. Growing up sucks.

Yes, it made me think of Mom again. I sighed and lowered my head. Stinky caught it and understood. "We'll save your mom."

I guess he can read minds, too.

"How about we go hide someplace?" I said. "And figure out what to do next."

He nodded. "I have a plan."

I sighed. "I know you do."

He held his arm out for me to take. In the middle of all of this, it was a cute and comforting thing for him to do. I took it. He walked me to the closet. No one noticed because people were still lingering and talking and leaving.

When we got there, he ditched his coat in the broom closet.

"Hey, what's wrong with us," I said. "Can't we hide in there, too?"

Stinky hit his head with his hand. "Duh," he said.

And sometimes he's clueless.

We must have sat in that closet for an hour, watching shadows move under the door and listening to the band pack up. How long does it take to pack an accordion and sixty out-of-tune saxophones anyway? Stinky made good use of the time, unwrapping one of the gifts. It was the staple gun and the fishing line.

I knew they'd show up at some point. I'd bought them but I still had no idea what they were for. I was starting to get too scared to ask, and sitting on the floor, my legs were getting cold.

Without saying a word, Stinky put his coat over them.

No longer clueless.

Finally, the lights went out. We waited a little longer, maybe twenty minutes where we didn't say a word to each other. Then Stinky whispered, "I'm going out, you stay here. Keep that other bucket ready in case I need you to use it." He slowly opened the door and crawled out, staple gun in his back pocket, the fishing line in his teeth. I closed the door behind him.

I sat in the dark and listened to him use that staple gun a bunch of times. Clack. Clack. Clack. I prayed the vampires wouldn't hear it. Then through the crack at the bottom of the door, I saw the lights go on.

Oh, no. They caught him, I whispered to myself. I didn't know what to do. Stinky was the one with the plan and he wasn't so good at sharing. To be honest, I didn't ask him for specifics either. One more thing to add to the list of things to do in the future, if I didn't get killed. Ask exactly what the plans are.

Plans or not, I had to do something. I stood up. Not easy.

My legs were cramped, and the heels didn't help. So, I took the heels off and had them in one hand. I picked up the bucket of holy water with the other hand, but it was shaking so much, it was splashing holy water out onto my bare feet. It was cold. Really cold. I opened the door a crack and peeked out. Stinky was sitting cross-legged in the middle of the dance floor, a vampire on either side of him. "You're Sandra's child, aren't you?" one of them said.

They didn't know I was a girl? Wow.

"Yeah, so what?" he answered back. He was protecting me. Sigh.

"Stefan has been looking for you. I'd kill you now, but I know he wants the pleasure. You and your friends have been a thorn in our sides, but no more. Now tell me where the others are hiding, and we won't make this painful."

"Others?" Stinky said. "There are no others. I came alone to save my mom. I've killed five of you blood boys already. You think you're bad. You aren't so bad."

"That's impossible," said the other one. "We're immortal."

Listening to this, I knew what I had to do. The question was, how? I could have rushed right out, but I didn't know where the other two vampires were. I couldn't see or hear them. I didn't even know if they were there.

"Your kind can cease to exist, believe me. As far as dying? Try looking in the mirror sometime. You're already dead." Stinky was really being nasty now.

The vampire kicked Stinky. Just hard enough to move him

a little across the slick floor. Stinky didn't even acknowledge it.

"Soon your mother will live forever, too," the first one said. "Once she's one of us, we'll be her family. She won't even remember you existed." They both laughed.

At that moment I stopped wondering where the other vampires were. I didn't care. I'd heard enough. I threw the door open in a rage. "You'll NEVER get my mother!" I screamed as I ran toward them, bucket ready. Both vampires turned to face me.

"Jess, WATCH YOUR FEET," Stinky yelled.

He had strung the fishing line across the floor to trip the vampires. It hadn't worked on them, but it worked great on me. I was running full speed when I hit the fishing line. The two vampires stood with their backs to Stinky as they watched me flying through the air. Instead of dropping the bucket and using my hands to break the fall, I thrust my arms forward and threw the water at the vampires.

At the same time, Stinky used both hands to shove them from behind, toward the oncoming water. I didn't even see the water hit them, because with my arms straight out in front of me, I landed right on my face. And it hurt.

I looked up to see two smoking figures squirming on the floor in front of me, until they weren't there anymore.

"Double play," Stinky yelled.

"I think I broke my nose," I said as I got up.

My face felt all wet. I looked down and saw blood dripping onto my new dress. My nose was bleeding like crazy. I put my hand up to try and stop it. I still had one shoe in my hand. I don't know where the other one went.

"I'll find you some napkins or something," Stinky said, running off.

"No, let it bleed," said a voice behind me.

It was one of the other vampires. He'd come out of nowhere.

I spun around and found myself face to face with him, his fangs at full length, his eyes wide. The blood from my nose was running down my chin and onto my dress, turning it bright red.

I felt all the energy drain from my body. I couldn't fight this guy. He was too strong. I was too tired. *At least we tried*, I thought.

He kept staring at the blood on my face. "I'll just tell Stefan I couldn't help myself. I know he wants you for himself, but I can't let all this beautiful blood go to waste. I know he'll understand." He grabbed my shoulders. This was it.

I closed my eyes and waited for the end.

"Hey FANG-FACE," screamed Stinky. "Try this one on for size."

My eyes went wide.

The vampire had concentrated so hard on me and my bloody nose that he had completely forgotten about Stinky. As he turned to look at Stinky, he loosened his grip on me slightly. It was enough for me to pull away and go down to the floor.

Stinky stood about ten or fifteen feet away swinging the jump rope over his head. He had used the clothes pins to attach five or six water balloons to it. The vampire didn't have any time to react. As soon as I went down, Stinky let the jump rope fly. As it wrapped itself around the vampire, the balloons broke one by one, soaking him in holy water.

He staggered around smoking and screaming for a second, then fell right on top of me. Now both of us were screaming. The next thing I knew I was lying on the floor alone, covered in vampire dust. And to top it off, I was at yet another level of scared. At least now I knew my heart was in good shape, because if it wasn't, it would have stopped right there. But—and this is the best part—I was still alive.

I lay there on the floor, trying to calm myself down until Stinky came over and put his hand out to help me up.

"I don't think Nanook and Sadie could ever have appreciated that present as much as you did," he said. The jump rope, clothes pins, and the balloons had been in the other package, ready to go, and they had saved my life. Stinky is a full-blown genius.

I took his hand and stood up. I had blood all over my face and chest and vampire dust in my hair and ears and in my eyes and probably between my toes. I was covered in it. My dress was destroyed. I lost one shoe and my grip on the other one was so tight from everything that had happened, you couldn't have pried it from me with a crowbar.

"You look bad," said Stinky, as he stood there in front of me, grinning. He didn't have a spot on him. I wanted to punch him and hug him at the same time.

"I feel like I got hit by a train," I said.

Suddenly, at a speed I have never seen a human move (okay, he wasn't human), the last vampire rushed out of nowhere at Stinky, knocking him so hard he went sliding across the floor and into the far wall. One second, he was there in front of me, the next, he was gone. I looked over at Stinky. He didn't move.

That vampire was breathing hard. Mad didn't come close to this animal's emotion right then. His eyes were crimson red. His fangs dripped with vampire venom. He moved to me, slowly. Stinky wasn't going to save me this time.

The vampire reached out and grabbed me. I put my hands up to block him. It didn't work. He was too quick and strong. He caught my hands and pulled me into him with great force.

Then, the weirdest thing in the world happened.

His eyes opened wide. Then they filled with tears. They spilled out and on to me. I used that moment to push myself away from him, hard. As I did, he looked at me and said, "Why?"

I stood there and looked at him. He was staring down at his chest. There in his chest was Mom's shoe, the one with the wood heels, with the heel buried in his flesh.

He looked so sad for a second, and then . . . whoooooosh.

Blue flames to the ceiling and across it, and he was gone. Mom's shoe fell to the floor and clacked on the shiny surface.

It was then I realized that when he pulled me in so hard, he stabbed himself with the wood heel on Mom's shoe. When I pushed him away, it went in further. It was dumb luck. Or not. I mean, I DID choose those shoes.

I was standing there, admiring my handiwork, when Stinky moaned. I ran over to him.

He sat up and looked at me. "What happened?"

"Nothing. Everything," I said.

"They all gone?" He looked so tired.

"All gone. You need to rest."

"No rest now, Jess," he said. "Stefan could be back any minute and we're out of ammo. We need to get out of here."

I helped him up and we limped out together. Well, after I went and got my purse from the closet. If later you asked me why I did that, I couldn't have told you. Stinky was great about it though. I still hadn't told him about the killer shoe, either.

We decided to go out the back way. It took us a while to find the back door, but once we did, we were out of there and back at Stinky's house in less than an hour. We were careful to stay in shadows as much as possible and be as quiet as we could all the way home. We didn't need Stefan or Leopold finding us now, with no way of protecting ourselves except for some garlic powder in my purse. Stefan and the other vampire were going to be mad enough when they got back to the State Building and saw what we'd done. And this time they were going to know who did it. There was no tomorrow.

And it was tomorrow.

April 13.

When we got back to Stinky's, Mrs. Van Helsing was sound asleep. I went straight to the shower. My dress was totally wrecked. It was covered in blood and vampire dust. And I left the vampire killing shoes at the party. Now, I owed Mom three hundred and seventy-five dollars.

Stinky found one of his mom's sweat suits for me to wear and a pair of her flip flops, so I wasn't barefoot. The sweat suit was little too big, but okay.

I looked at the dress. The only dress I'd ever loved. The dress that got Brad to come say hi to me. But then it occurred to me that it was just a thing. Not important when you thought about everything else that was at stake. I put it in the trash can in Stinky's room. Thank you, dress.

Stinky, who is fearless, was already asleep. Nothing must bother him. I sat up for a while. As I sat there, I looked over at Stinky, lying there in bed snoring, and wondered how we were going to get out of this. This was no dream. It was all too real. I was afraid. I was afraid for Mom. I was afraid for Dad. I was even afraid for Lily. Let's face it, I was afraid for everybody. Strange though, I wasn't really afraid for me. Just everyone else. Maybe because I had faced the end and accepted it, and then the randomness of the high heel cheating death, or maybe because I realized I'd gladly give up my life for Mom and Dad. Did I want to? Heck no. Not even close. Not without a fight. But I would. Is this adulthood?

I didn't know how we could win. We hadn't finished the job and we weren't anonymous anymore. They knew who we were, and my mom was on their side.

There was no doubt about it. Stefan wanted me dead. Us dead. I'd heard it from his mouth myself. We now had a two hundred and fifty year old vampire thirsting for our blood, looking for revenge. And after he saw what we did to his vampire family, I knew he would stop at nothing to get us, and my whole family. Stinky's, too, probably. It was clear our days of surprise attacks were over. He was going to be ready for us from now on.

I started thinking about what he's done to Mom. My eyes filled with tears. Those vampires said Mom wouldn't even remember me.

Mom used to come in at night, sit on the edge of my bed, and we'd just talk about anything and everything. School, friends, Lily, just stuff, it didn't matter. She was always interested in what I had to say, even if it was stupid or wrong. And she didn't get mad at stuff that she thought was bad; she just explained quietly why she thought it was wrong and loved me no matter what. I needed that in my life, and it was gone. I felt totally lost. Dad was my only hope now. I still had him. I prayed that by now he'd read my letter and most of all, believed it.

Only two to go. The worst two.

I must have fallen asleep sitting up because I woke up in a weird position and also, I hurt all over.

I got up, stretched, and looked at myself in the mirror. Not good. I looked in Stinky's desk for a rubber band and put my ponytail back in.

Stinky's mother didn't even blink when she saw me in the morning. It was like this was a natural occurrence. She just offered me breakfast. I don't think she even noticed I was wearing her clothes.

"You have girls overnight a lot?" I asked Stinky.

He laughed. "Are you kidding? NO. You're the first sleepover here ever, boy or girl, and I think Mom is excited that I have a friend. Any friend. She's just being cool about it." He looked at me. "We are friends, right?"

"Of course we are," I said. "Best friends. But we do have a lot to talk about later, though."

After a delicious breakfast of eggs and what looked like lawn clippings, I thanked Stinky's mom and got ready to go home. The sun was up.

We left Stinky's and headed back to my house. We got a little way down the sidewalk and his Mom ran out of the house after us, waving my purse. "Sweetie!! You forgot this!"

I took it from her and thanked her. We continued our walk to my house.

We walked without talking for a while.

"I've been thinking," I said. "We need to go in the back door when we get home. Stefan might have called Mom and she could be waiting at the front for us."

"Smart," Stinky said.

We walked some more.

"We have all day to figure out what to do next," Stinky finally said. "They can't come for us until after dark, so we have time to get ready. They won't know what hit them."

"Stinky, please, please don't get too confident. I've thought a lot about this. Stefan has got to be beyond mad and he's going to be careful because he knows we know how to kill them. He's not just going to walk into one of your traps. Stefan's not dumb. You may have plans, but you better believe so will he."

We walked in silence some more. I checked inside my purse for the garlic powder and nervously played with the screw top.

My mom bought that powder after she was bitten the second time. Maybe there was hope. Maybe this powder would help me save her.

And then there was Dad. Oh, Dad. He was in my thoughts, too. And not just about the vampire thing.

"What are you thinking about?" Stinky asked.

"Oh, come on. I've been gone all night. No, not gone. Missing. I never did that before. My dad must be going crazy worrying about me. Mom? She'll be surprised to see me alive, I think. I'm having a lot of problems wrapping my head around all of this. What do we tell him? Or her?"

"Doesn't matter. She knows only what Stefan wants her to know. Nothing we say can change that."

"And my dad? He's liable to kill you himself for making him worry about me all night. He'll see me in this get-up and wonder where my dress is. I promise that. It's an Olympic-gold-medal mess."

"It'll be okay."

"Really? You don't get it. We, together, have got to tell Dad everything, if he hasn't read the letter, and somehow prove to him that we're telling the truth."

"You wrote him a letter?"

"I did. I told him everything. We can't fight these guys alone. We're in way over our heads."

"Speak for yourself," Stinky said. "We don't need to tell your dad anything. We can do this. I. Have. A. Plan."

We had reached the back door of my house by this time. "Another plan?" I said. "Guaranteed to work?"

"Guaranteed," he said.

"This time I'll need to know exactly what it is. Okay?"

"Absolutely." He was smiling.

I looked at the back door. "I don't have a key. I hope Dad answers," I told him.

I went to knock, but before I could, Stinky tried the door. It was unlocked. It's never unlocked unless someone is in the backyard working and can see it. I looked at Stinky. "This isn't good."

"They can't come for us until tonight. Relax."

He entered in front of me. It was completely dark inside. Mom's new drapes and shades were working well. The sun through the back door lit up the kitchen. Nobody was in there.

I closed the door. *Where is everybody?* I wondered.

Stinky said, "Let's get some light in here."

"Good idea. I've had enough of this darkness stuff to last a million years." I searched with my hand in the dark for the kitchen light and flipped it on.

There were plates on the kitchen table, full of half eaten food.

"I'm telling you, I don't like this," I said.

"Hey. You haven't overreacted up to this point. Don't start now."

We went through the kitchen door and into the living room. It was pitch dark. Stinky found a lamp and turned it on. There, sitting on the sofa, were Stefan, Leopold and Mom. Stefan smiled and waved hello.

Stinky looked at me. "Okay, you can overreact."

He turned to run back into the kitchen, but Leopold sprang up from the sofa and knocked him to the floor. "Move and I will kill you now," he said, and then hissed. Stinky didn't move. I froze where I was.

"You have caused me an awful lot of trouble," Stefan said quietly. "My family is almost destroyed, and who is responsible? Two little kids?" He was up and yelling now. "Two snot-nosed little kids? I haven't had this much interference in two hundred years. Someone must pay." He was standing right in front of me now, screaming in my face.

"How did you get in here?" I asked him. "I put garlic on all the windows and doors last night."

I pulled the jar from my purse and looked at it. Why hadn't it worked? There on the label was the reason. I had never looked at it closely. It said, imitation garlic powder. I should have known Mom would never buy the real stuff. And now I was going to die because I didn't remember to go to the store.

I dropped the jar at Stefan's feet.

I had to think of something. Stinky didn't have a plan for this. He was still on the floor at Leopold's feet. I looked around the room. There on a side table was Dad's briefcase and it was open.

The letter, I thought. Oh, no. Stefan read the letter. Dad's probably dead and it's my fault. Oh . . . and Lily. What happened to Lily? It was panic time.

Mom showed no emotion at all. "Mom?" I said to her. "Where's Dad and Lily? Did you let these jerks get Dad and

Lily?" I was yelling now.

"No, honey," she said. She wasn't even looking at me. She was looking at Stefan to see if she could answer. He was now in complete control. He nodded for her to go on. "Your father took Lily somewhere last night and I haven't seen them since."

He was alive. Dad was alive.

"We'll wait here until your father comes back. We'll take care of him after we deal with you and that Van Helsing kid," Stefan said, pointing at Stinky. He said the name, Van Helsing, with as much hate as I have ever heard. But I couldn't worry about Stinky now. He was here. I had to worry about the rest of my family that wasn't.

"And what about Lily?" I asked Stefan.

"Lily will join your mother and me in building a new family. You took care of the old one. Lily's too young to be turned yet, but she'll live the life as one of us, and when she's old enough, she'll look forward to joining us."

"I hate you," I said calmly, "and someone, someday, will stop you."

"You won't be around to see it," Leopold said. "But you will be around long enough to see me drain all the blood from your friend. You watched my friends die. Now you can watch your friend die."

He reached down and picked Stinky up by the neck. Stinky struggled against him for a second. It was no use. Leopold giggled for a moment, then opened his mouth, bared his fangs, and started to bite Stinky's neck. It was horrible to see.

At that moment, the door to the kitchen burst open.

It was Dad!

"NO! NO! NO!" Dad screamed. He had a wooden broom in his hands. The end of it was in a point. He rushed at Leopold, who threw Stinky against the wall. Stinky hit hard and slid down, out cold.

Stefan moved to stop Dad. As he got in front of me, I stuck my foot out and tripped him. He fell on the coffee table, breaking it.

While this was going on, Dad took the broomstick handle, and using it as a ram, shoved Leopold against the wall. Then with a grunt, he forced the sharpened wooden handle straight through Leopold's heart. Leopold burst into huge blue flames that streaked across the ceiling—and then he was gone.

"No!" screamed Stefan.

"Jess, get out!" Dad yelled.

Before Dad could say another word, Stefan jumped over the sofa so fast he was a blur, and with one hand, he knocked Dad against the wall. Dad slid down, unconscious.

Boy, was Stefan mad. He looked up at the ceiling and he howled. So loud, it hurt my ears.

He stopped and then looked at Stinky who was still leaning against the wall. Stinky didn't move. Stefan looked at me and Mom, his eyes raging. He looked down at Dad. You could see him thinking. It wasn't good.

While Stefan was focused on my Dad, I grabbed Mom's hand. "Let's go!" I yelled. It was like pulling on a statue. I pulled hard a couple of times before I gave up and ran toward the front door. Before I could get to it, Stefan caught me from behind and spun me around. "You did this to me," he said in a rage. "You've destroyed two centuries of my work."

I looked around him at Mom. She sat still on the sofa, staring off into space. "Mom," I begged, "please help me. Look at Dad. How can you let this happen?"

She turned and looked at me. For the first time, there were tears in her eyes. "You don't understand, honey. There's nothing I can do. It's too late."

"Listen to your mother, Jessica," Stefan said, grinning at me. "Mom always knows best."

I'd had enough. *Enough.* I wound up and slugged him in the chest as hard as I could. Harder than I'd hit Rocco. It actually backed him up a bit. He was stunned. Not by the blow, but the fact that I did it, I think. Plus, now my hand hurt.

He laughed. "Too little, too late," Stefan said, his voice oozing with fake sympathy.

And he was right. It was too late for all of us. I couldn't help Stinky, or Dad, or Lily. Or Mom. Poor Mom, I could see how much this was hurting her. It was in her face. It wasn't her fault. If Mom had any control, she would have been fighting this guy with me.

I looked her in the eye. "I love you anyways, Mom. No matter what you do."

"Anyways isn't a word," she said back. Holy crap. Mom was still in there somewhere!

Stefan spun me around to face him again.

"Do you have anything to say, before I have breakfast?" he asked me.

Very funny—I was breakfast.

"I do have a question," I said.

He nodded his head. "Fair enough. Ask." He let me go.

"How did you get here? I thought you guys couldn't go out during the day."

"We've been waiting here since last night," he said. "As long as we stay out of the sunlight, we can move any time of day. Your mother has equipped this house beautifully. Not a drop of sunlight comes in through those windows now. I would love to keep this place, but we can't have the authorities finding your bodies the way I will leave them."

"Stinky says you'll burn down the house," I said.

"He's a Van Helsing. He knows," Stefan said, looking down at Stinky, who was still lying motionless on the floor against the wall. "Fire hides a lot of sins."

"Let my father live," I said. "Please? You can do anything you want to me."

"Your mother has another life now—with me. Your father would just be in the way. In a few days, I can bite her for the third time, completing her transformation. Then together we'll build a new family. And in time, and we have a lot of it you know, we will control this city. Now say goodbye to your mother." He grabbed my shoulders.

I looked at Mom again. She was still on the sofa, but tears

were now streaming down her face. I looked at Dad, unconscious on the floor. I looked at Stinky. I looked around the room and there on the floor, in a corner with his nose in one of my tennis shoes, was Half-Whit. Unbelievable. He'd slept through the whole thing. I couldn't believe that stupid dog was the last thing I was ever going to see.

"Well, good-bye Half-Whit," I said.

"What?" Stefan said, a puzzled look on his face. He loosened his grip a little.

"Not you," I said. "My dog, Whitman."

Of course. Whitman. How could I be so blind?

The room spun around me. With all my might, I pulled away from Stefan and screamed, "WHITMAN, SUNLIGHT!"

That squatty little dog jumped up just like Grandma taught him, rushed to the drapes, grabbed a corner, and started to pull them open.

"Stop him!" screamed Stefan, but it was too late. Sunlight poured into the room.

Stefan looked at me with terror in his eyes and started shaking. Sunlight covered his whole body now. His skin started blistering. I grabbed Mom, pulling her off the sofa.

Stefan's body was popping and hissing and shaking uncontrollably. I threw Mom on the floor and jumped on top of her.

At that instant, Stefan exploded in a flash of bright light. The blast blew all the windows out of the house. All the doors flew off, a big part of the roof flew off, and the chimney cracked.

Mom and I lay there on the floor for a while. She was out

cold, maybe from the shock of being released from Stefan's power. That's what I hoped, at least.

I finally got up and looked around the room. The furniture was all turned over and broken. Thank goodness there was no broken glass anywhere. It must have all been blown outside. I looked up and saw the sky where the roof had been. It was now probably in the street. The house was destroyed. But my family was alive.

And there, in the corner, was Half-Whit, asleep again with his nose in my shoe.

I love that dog.

I could hear sirens in the distance. Someone must have called the fire department after the explosion. I didn't care. I felt wonderful. It was the best day of my life. We blew up the head vampire. Me . . . and my dog. My magnificent dog.

And I had my mom back.

Stinky moved and groaned. I ran to help him up. He looked around the room. "What happened?" he asked. "Are you hurt?" He was thinking of me first.

"Pish tosh," I said, and I leaned in and kissed him on the forehead. It seemed like the right thing to do.

"Are we in heaven?" he asked. I laughed.

"We won. Stefan and Leopold are dead," I said.

"How?" he asked. "The last thing I remember is a set of oversized fangs."

"My dad and my dog," I said proudly.

"Your dog?"

"I'll tell you later. We have company," I said, as the firemen came through where the front door used to be.

Cops and EMTs and firemen. It was another convention. This time I couldn't be happier to see them. Stinky refused any treatment and told them to take care of Mom and Dad.

They took Mom and Dad and me and Lily to the hospital in an ambulance. Stinky told me he'd take Half-Whit . . . Whitman . . . to his house until we came home, or wherever we'd have to go since our house was blown up.

At the hospital the cops asked Dad and me all kinds of questions. They tried to ask Mom, but she was really out of it. Dad and I said the explosion came as a complete surprise. Out of nowhere. Well, Dad said it first, and then looked at me to make sure our stories were going to be the same. They were. We both lied.

In the end, the doctors said we were all okay. Dad had a minor concussion and Mom was Mom again. And the cops stopped asking questions, so that was good. We did look pretty innocent.

At the hospital, when Mom finally came around a little, she was more concerned about Dad and me than she was about herself. It was great. Everything else was fuzzy for her, she said.

Later, we all left the hospital together, a family again, and we went home. Or what was left of home.

April 14.

We ended up at a real nice hotel. We had a suite. It was sooo great. Lily and I got our own room. It had internet, cable TV, room service, and a big swimming pool downstairs. The maids cleaned up everything and made our beds. It was major cool.

Dad said our homeowner's insurance policy was paying for everything, so go ahead and pig out on room service. And we did.

Some of the kids from school came by that first day and said I was famous because my house blew up. And that everybody in town drove by to look at it. A picture of it was even on the Internet. Our house trended for a day. My friends said it was major great. So, maybe I'll be more popular now.

I'm not sure I want that though.

When I was downstairs checking out the pool later, Rocco came by to see if I was okay. He'd heard about the house, too. I asked him if he remembered that night with the vampires. He shook a little and said he kinda did and knew I saved his life and now he was in debt to me forever. I figured it was like I pulled a thorn out of his paw, or something. Nobody at high school is ever messing with me again. Well, if Rocco made it out of junior high.

As he left, he said, "See ya, Trueheart." This time he said it with affection. It worked.

I waved my hand at him, "Pish tosh," I answered. I'll bet he thought it was French or something.

After Lily and Mom were asleep, Dad and I were in the living area of the suite. I knew he needed to talk. We hadn't had time alone to talk about everything since Stefan made our roof blow into outer space. "You should have told me from the beginning," he said, sitting with me on the sofa.

"Come on Dad, vampires? You wouldn't have believed me. You would've laughed."

"Hey, you should be glad I did end up believing you. I found your letter Saturday night, when I was getting something from my briefcase. At first, I thought it was the most ridiculous story I'd ever read."

"Thanks a lot."

He put his hand on my shoulder. "Please don't take this wrong, Jess, but the more I thought about what you had written the more I knew it had to be true. Not only because it explained your mother's strange behavior, but also because you got a D in creative writing last year and there was so much intricate detail to everything you wrote. You just couldn't make something like this up. And don't get too comfy with it—it's the last time I'll be happy if you get a D in anything." He was smiling now. Plus, He remembered it was only a D. Yay!

"What did you do after that? Were you scared?" I asked him.

"Kind of, at the beginning. And a lot, later. To make sure I wasn't crazy to believe you, I got a mirror and tried to get your mom's reflection in it and couldn't. She was there, but her reflection wasn't. That's when I grabbed Lily and got out of the house. I took her to Aunt Gina's and came back to fight for your mom. I'm so glad you wrote about the stakes through the heart thing. That's where the broom came from. You."

"You did great, Dad," I said. "You saved us."

"No honey," he said, smiling. "You saved your mom, you and Abraham, if everything you wrote in that letter is true."

"And Half-Whit," I said proudly. "I love that dog."

"I'm not sure I understand that yet," Dad said.

"No need to, Dad. Just a special bond between a girl and her dog."

Dad laughed. "Well, I'm very proud of you. You were braver than I ever could be. One thing though, not a word of this to your mother. Ever. It has to be our secret."

When the doctors talked to Mom at the hospital, she had no memory of the last few of months. Night school, Stefan, vampires, all gone. The doctor told her the explosion had affected her short-term memory. We let her believe that.

April 15.

Dad got me a cell phone. He said I earned it. YAY!!!!!

April 20.

Still at the hotel. Stinky was missing. I hadn't talked to him since that day. He wasn't at school either. When I called his house, nothing. Dad and I went by after school a couple of times. It was dark. He was missing and so was my dog. Not good. Dad said not to worry, but I did.

April 29.

Still no news from Stinky. And he'd never been back to school.

April 30.

The insurance company finished their investigation of the

explosion and said it was caused by a "weather related temperature and air pressure inversion," whatever that is. Dad didn't care—he was just glad that they were going to pay up. He didn't think he was covered for exploding vampires.

He told the workers to fix it right away, anyways. Anyway.

We finally got to go home, too. No more swimming pools, room service or maids. We were going to have to make our own beds again.

All the windows had been replaced, the roof was fixed, there were doors, and the foundation of the house had been checked. The chimney was still cracked. Dad told them not to fix it. I think he wanted to keep it like that as a reminder.

When we got to the front door there was a cardboard delivery box on the porch. Mom picked it up. She smiled, then looked at me. "It's for you," she said, handing it to me.

It was. No return address. Nice, typed label. Okay.

I took it to my room and threw it on my bed, and then I went out to help carry all our stuff back into the house.

It wasn't until the afternoon that I sat down on my bed and opened the box. Inside of it was the dress. My dress. The dress. All clean. I pulled it out and looked at it. It looked beautiful. An envelope fell to the floor. I picked it up. My name was printed on the front, in crayon. I laughed. I put the dress, my dress, on the bed and opened it.

It was a letter from Stinky. He'd gotten home from the biggest vampire explosion in years and his mom immediately put him and Whitman in her car and drove them to Idaho. Idaho?

Mrs. Van Helsing's mom had a stroke and they had to go take care of her. Stinky said his mom didn't even ask him until they were in Idaho a couple of days where Whitman came from. At least she's consistent.

He'd grabbed the dress before they left and had it cleaned like new for me in Idaho. The cleaners even got the blood stains out. He said I looked too pretty in it to throw it away. Awww.

He said he didn't know where we were to call me. That's true. I didn't have my cell phone until afterward. By the way, did I tell you I now have a cell phone?

He also said his grandma finally died. So, we have something else in common now; and he said he'd be home by the time I got this, probably.

I used my cell phone to call his house. His mom answered and said Stinky was out back playing with her dog. Her dog? Okay. Not good.

So, I walked to Stinky's to get Whitman. My dog. Mrs. Van Helsing didn't want him to leave. She said that Whitman was the only dog she'd ever really understood. As much as I love him now, I didn't understand that. At all. But I told her she could play with him anytime she wanted. Then Whitman farted. Mrs. Van Helsing didn't care. Somehow, that made sense to me.

Stinky and I couldn't really talk about what happened because his mom still didn't know anything.

But when we got outside as I was leaving, Stinky said he'd heard that the old State Building had already been leased to a bunch of doctors for a clinic. He was going to make sure they were really doctors. I didn't ask him how.

We decided to get together the next day and catch up. I had a LOT to tell him and to thank him for.

May 1.

I was rummaging through the kitchen cupboard looking for food. Mom grabbed me from behind and scared me. I was still jumpy.

"Hey, I'm making dinner. You'll spoil your appetite."

"Right," I said, as I heard a knock at the back door.

I walked over and opened it. Stinky walked into the kitchen like he didn't have a care in the world. "Hey," he said.

"Hey," I answered back.

Mom looked at him and then at me. "And who is this?"

The question startled me. Then I realized that she had only met Stinky after she had been bitten. She had no idea who he was.

"I'm Abraham Van Helsing," he said, shaking her hand. "Very nice to meet you, Mrs. Scott."

"Wow," she said. "A polite one. You could learn a lot from this one, Jess."

"I already have, Mom," I said, smiling. Plus, the new non-vampire Mom didn't call me Jessica anymore. That was nice.

I sniffed the air. Garlic?

"Mom? What's for dinner?" I asked.

"Spaghetti and garlic bread," she said. "Would your friend like to stay?"

"I'd love to, Mrs. Scott," Stinky answered.

I almost broke my face I was smiling so hard.

At dinner, Dad and Stinky finally got to know each other officially. Dad now knew the truth, so he stopped hating Stinky so much. Plus, I found out that Dad had an insect collection as a kid. They bonded over bugs.

After dinner, Stinky and I went for a walk. His dad was coming home soon and Stinky couldn't wait to tell him what happened. At least he had somebody to tell. Dad said I'd better not tell anybody unless I wanted to get sent to a psych ward for a mental examination.

Stinky scared me though. He said he was studying up on werewolves after hearing that vampire mention them. I told him I didn't want to hear anything about it. I even covered my ears.

I brought Half-Whit along on our walk. I had to drag him a little and carry him a lot, but nothing is too good for that dog.

Later, I tried to show Stinky how Half-Whit saved us, but no matter how much I yelled, Whitman wouldn't go near the drapes for me. I guess he didn't want to show off.

Dad came in the living room while Mom was cleaning the kitchen and Lily was watching TV and shook Stinky's hand. "Thank you, son," he said. That's it. That's all he said. But you could see in Dad's eyes everything he wanted to say.

"My pleasure," is all Stinky said back. They'd never have to talk about it again.

When Stinky left to go home, he looked all sad and stuff.

"What's wrong," I asked him.

He kicked the ground. "Will you still want to hang out with me now that your mom is okay?"

I kissed him on the cheek. "Pish tosh."

He grinned. "See you tomorrow?"

"I'm counting on it." Then, I swear he was skipping as I watched him go down the sidewalk.

Yep, it was great to be home and great to have Mom be Mom. After I went to bed, she came in and sat with me for a while. She put her arms around me, she stroked my hair, and she was interested in everything I had to say, no matter how stupid or wrong it was. We talked about school, friends, Lily, and anything else I wanted, too.

Well . . . almost anything

THE END

www.ingramcontent.com/pod-product-compliance
Lightning Source LLC
LaVergne TN
LVHW010058110826
845155LV00028B/399

* 9 7 8 1 9 4 1 0 1 5 7 4 2 *